A BU

Gentlemen of the Coast Book 3

by
Danielle Thorne

Quote

"DeLuna was enthusiastic about the place and he told the Crown that his seamen believed it to be 'the best port in the Indies.' He wrote that the country 'seems to be healthy. It is somewhat sandy, from which I judge that it will not yield much bread. There are pine trees, live oaks, and many other kinds of trees.' De Luna said little about the natives because there were very few of them and those who showed up were quite friendly. He identified them as 'only a few fishermen.'"[1]

— Charles W. Arnade
The Florida Historical Quarterly

CHAPTER ONE

Pensacola, La Florida
1796

PHILLIP OAKLEY WALKED the sandy path to the Spanish settlement in the darkness knowing it by heart. The comforting scent of seagrass and pine filled his senses and almost made him feel at home. He'd walked this land as a captive in British-controlled Pensacola until England lost the revolution in America and moved him to the Indies. There, he'd flourished as a fisherman and bought a small boat. When his business took off, his history was forgotten. He was a rich man now. No one cared where he lived, or how.

A sudden burst of laughter exploded in the air, and Phillip froze. To his right, a loud voice replied, and he realized he'd stumbled past a late night conversation between two persons too important to keep quiet for the neighbors. He slunk against a shadowy tree to listen. Estimating how far he'd traveled from the bayou, he presumed it was one of the night watchmen near the officials' offices and homes. Someone said, "the gardens," in Spanish, and he heard fading footsteps to the north.

Phillip didn't wait to see if they were leaving for the settlement's gardens in the other direction. He darted down a fork in the path on the tips of his boots trying to be as stealthy as possible. At most, they would think it was a rabbit in the brush.

It would not do for the American owner of the *Mary Alice* to be spotted slinking around town on the same day Captain Redbird had pirated a trading ship and relieved it of its cargo. The *Mary Alice* had sailed into Pensacola harbor good and proper, but no one had seen Phillip Oakley make his way off because he hadn't been aboard. Captain Page and his crew would swear he was, but the men knew he'd sailed their secret sister ship—the *Revenge*—into the nearby bayou with those who wanted to pirate.

The path ended at thick mounds of sand. Phillip crept out of a small grove of trees onto the beach just east of the harbor. Waves bounced lazily onto the sand except for strange stalking and rhythmic splashes in the surf. He squinted in the weak moonlight until his eyes focused on a person wading through the shallows. There was a squeal, and his heart jumped. A long curtain of hair swung across a woman's shoulders as she bent over in the water. Was she hurt? One could step on a whipray or pinching crab if not careful.

Without thinking, Phillip strode across the narrow stretch of beach and charged into the water from behind. She spun, and he saw a flash of teeth when she opened her mouth to scream. He slapped his hand over her lips before she could and pinned her against his chest.

She was a small thing. A dressing gown shimmered like silk under flashes of moonbeams, and he knew this was no fisherman's wife. Her forehead came up to his lips, he realized, when they brushed over her skin. The lady grabbed him by the sleeves of his shirt and pushed and when that didn't work, squealed in fear. He sensed claws coming for his face and reached up with practiced ease and grabbed a wrist. Her other hand grabbed a handful of his cheek, and she pinched until her fingernails sank into his flesh. Phillip winced, pushed her away, then scooped her up in one arm and hurried for the tree line.

"Quiet," he hissed, his mind scrambling between his two identities. If he was discovered, neither would matter because he'd be a corpse in the hangman's noose if they didn't shoot him.

The woman became still, and he cupped the hand he held over her mouth so she didn't bite him. He prayed she was a lady's maid with whom he was mildly acquainted; someone who would not look down on him and believe his story. She let go of his cheek and clubbed him in the ear.

"Ow," he whispered. She stiffened. Phillip strained to hear if voices were raised in alarm in the distance. Only the tide answered. He loosed his grip enough to let her feet slide down to the sand. Her rumpled robe came all undone, and she snatched at the hems to yank it shut.

"I mean you no harm," he said in a polite tone but held fast to her shoulder while his other hand smothered any possible screams. "I'm not drunk, and I'm nobody's enemy." That was a complicated but necessary falsehood.

The woman smelled like lavender and fruit. He squinted in the darkness, and seeing nothing, backed her against a sturdy tree trunk. "I'm going to let go of you, and you are not going to run or strike me. Do we have an agreement?"

In the dim moonlight, he saw her dark features nod. Phillip let go of her wrist. He felt her lips move and hot breath against his hand and realized she was terrified. He wanted to assure her he'd never harmed a woman, but the sword at his side suggested differently. Instead, he whispered, "I was just out walking, Miss..."

Phillip realized he'd revealed himself with the outburst in English. Many of his crew were former British subjects or free men of color. English was the language aboard both his legal merchantman and the swift pirating schooner.

"*Mwa nwan his bamessuh mmtwmdoo*," the lady mumbled through his fingers.

"Shh!" He looked around, heart clomping. "I'm going to let you go, and you're going to walk straight back to your home without looking back. Do you understand?"

An assembly of leaves ruffled overhead. A storm was brewing from out of nowhere as they often did. His prisoner shivered. She felt warm against him and smelled like an afternoon in heaven. Phillip strained to see her. The muddled clouds shifted enough for him to make out a feminine face with round cheekbones. His breath gnarled in his chest as his mind sorted through the buildings and haciendas on this side of the settlement. Her hacienda would be a house fine enough to provide its lady with such a garment.

Montego! The stiff, stern, and official abode of Don Marcos Montego was one of the nearest officials' homes. Of course, he should have known her. There could not be more than six hundred people in Pensacola. This was the petite daughter of the don, who had come to Pensacola not long after the Spanish took possession of it from the British army.

Phillip's mind flitted through pictures of a young lady in the Montego carriage. Quiet and solemn, she attended official functions as a lone jewel. She belonged in Madrid at court, he thought, although there was something about her mixed-in Englishness that stood out like a bruise. She looked more like an American governor's daughter than a noblewoman in New Spain—oh, he'd seen his share. No wonder the don did not return home to *España*. It was clear she was a pebble in his shoe he'd picked up during his service abroad.

The woman pushed again, and he let her go, nerves clenched should she scream out for help. He would have to sprint into the underbrush and forget about returning to his rented room near the gardens. Her shadowy figure darted up the footpath, and to his relief, did not cry out. Phillip waited a few moments, shuffling his feet and looking down in surprise when his boot heel crunched. He bent over and studied a small pile of assorted shells. There was a pair of slippers, too. Looking back at the water, it all came together. It was a languid night. The surf was calm. No one was about. Why not go wading and exploring? But half-dressed?

Picking up the shells, Phillip crept down the path with his ears strained for suspicious activity. Miss Montego was so frightened she'd probably run straight home and back to bed. Surely the grim Don Marcos did not permit her to wander around at night.

Phillip quickened his pace and moved up the path until he reached the back of a grand courtyard camouflaged by large tropical palms and orange trees. From the shadows, he watched the shape of the woman slink up to the back hacienda door. He caught a glimpse of her from the glow of a smoldering torch before she slipped inside. Dark, rich hair draped in sheets over her shoulders past her lower back. There was a pleasing contrast between her fine satin robe now slid off her shoulder and a dusky-fair complexion.

He was right. This was no servant girl. He knew the soft-angled face and curved chin. It was the mysterious child of the don. Señorita Montego—or Miss Emma Montego—if they were on American soil. Who had not admired her? She was one of the few and finest ladies of the settlement.

Phillip stuck an arm through the bars of the gate and set down her shells and slippers. He then urged his boots to continue up the footpath until it split into a more traveled, rugged trail. Hurrying toward the little village of platform homes, he inhaled tilled earth and struggling vegetables.

The clouds in the sky moved along at a sharper pace, and the distant moon flashed between their breaks in the sky. A low growl of thunder sounded in the distance. *Almost there.* Phillip rented the second half of a sturdy cabin from a pleasant widow who did his laundry and saw to his meals. His side of the home had a low log fence, and he could be indoors within minutes if the night watch did not stand between him and safety.

He forced himself to calm as perspiration trickled down his back beneath his shirt. The storm would wash all traces of him and his arrival away. No one would be the wiser that the pirate Redbird had dropped anchor in the bayou, or that Phillip Oakley was not in port to do business but hiding from pirate hunters at sea.

EMMA MONTEGO FORCED herself awake and found it late morning. She sat up with a groan and ran her fingers through her tangled hair. She should never have unbraided it. She shouldn't have traipsed outside in the middle of the night for fresh air and seashells, either.

Her heart hurdled over a beat at the memory of her near-attack, and she squeezed her eyes shut. No wonder it was late. She'd hardly slept at all fearing the intruder would creep into the yard and come into the house after her. She'd only glimpsed him in the darkness—tall, dark hat, light-colored tunic, and wearing scents of tar and sun and seawater. She flushed at the memory of his soft mouth against her forehead. No beard either.

She shook herself from the shock of it. He was English, she was sure of it, and there weren't many here. Some had stayed when the Spaniards arrived. Their connections to the pelt trade and peaceful relationships with the natives made them too valuable to run out.

Voices drifted upstairs. Even though the voices were low, Emma could make out their frustrated tones expressing dismay to her father—a noble and titled don who commanded respect from everyone in the Pensacola settlement. She herself spoke *español* haltingly although it'd been five years since her life in Charleston ended with an abrupt knock on the door of the family who'd raised her since she was a baby. In that moment, a hundred questions had been answered but none of them satisfied.

Emma kicked down the thin coverlet. Don Marcos was no doubt discussing yesterday's hysterical gossip downstairs in the drawing room. From what she could understand between the floorboards, Captain Redbird, a pirate known to pillage British ships around the Indies, had attacked a Spanish trader nearby. Pensacola's merchants were up in arms.

The front door of the hacienda opened, and Emma listened to the settlement's powerful men drift out to their horses. Footsteps sounded on the stairs, and Emma scurried out of bed to get dressed. Someone knocked on the door. "Yes?"

Her only friend and companion, Roseline, slipped inside with her brows raised. "Are you ill?"

"No." Emma gave a sharp shake of her head. "I couldn't sleep with the heat and then there was that storm," she explained to her companion.

"Yes, it woke me, too," admitted Roseline in her choppy English. She set down a pile of shells and a pair of Emma's slippers. "Betsy found these in the courtyard."

"Oh, thank you," cried Emma, but it trailed off to a whisper. The shells did not look familiar. The slippers were the ones she'd taken off at the shore last night. Heart hammering, she glanced up, but Roseline had looked away.

"In the courtyard, you say?"

"Yes," chuckled her friend. "You must have left them outside after taking them to the courtyard to admire, but why your slippers?"

Roseline turned, and Emma gave her a bright, innocent smile. "I have no idea. My toes do get warm in those old things." Roseline smiled as she scattered a few seashells around the room as Emma liked to do.

Emma couldn't move. The man at the shore had followed her home. Those were her shoes and about the number of shells she'd picked up at the shore. Her stomach shrank, and she pushed her breakfast tray away. No one could know she'd snuck out. She glanced at the lock on her door with trembling hands and wondered if it would keep out a strange man.

Grains of sand still clung to her feet from the midnight scuffle when Emma reappeared from the other side of her privacy panel after washing. With a deep breath, she forced her fears aside while Roseline laced her into short stays then draped a clean petticoat over her head. The thin linen protected her skin but was light enough so she didn't suffocate in the Florida heat.

Roseline raked a comb through her tangled locks, brushed in a smudge of wax, then wove three sections into thick braids and coiled them up prettily on top of her head. Small ruby earbobs from the don were the only jewelry she chose.

Emma cringed when she looked at the bounty of pearls and gemstones stuffed into her trinket box with her shells. It made her blush to see others in Pensacola exhausting themselves to fish and hunt or scrabble in the sandy soil to grow whatever vegetables they could manage. She'd once done so in Charleston when she lived with the McKay family, but now she slept in a curtained European bed fit for a princess with gowns of East Indian silk and the glittering jewel box at her bedside. It still felt pretend—and wrong.

"Your papa wants to see you in his study when you are ready," murmured Roseline. She swept past Emma to pick up the breakfast tray to take down to Betsy.

"What is on the schedule today?" wondered Emma aloud. "I planned to go over the ledger in the kitchen with Adelaide."

"Just the usual rounds, although I think the don has a meeting at the armory."

Emma scrunched her brows. "What for? Who's come into port?"

"Hmm? Oh, no one, but..." Roseline hesitated. "Well, you will hear soon enough. Another ship was attacked in the gulf—one of Señor Peña's ships on its way to Havana."

"A trading ship?"

"Sí. No one was harmed. Only goods were taken."

Emma allowed one last appraisal of herself in the looking glass and found her skin sallow and uninteresting in the clean, white linen. She did not have velvety skin like Roseline or the smooth complexions of her Spanish neighbors. She was as sallow as an old sea cake washed up broken on the shore. A sudden thought pierced her vain regrets. "Pirates?"

"It was. How bold, sí?" Roseline opened the door while balancing the tray and yesterday's linens. "It was the *Revenge*. She flew an American flag, and they had no idea until it was too late."

Emma had not concerned herself with pirates in the past, not settled inside one of Florida's most protected ports. Pensacola was shielded by a peninsula on one side and a barrier island on the other. There was just a small gateway into the harbor, and the allowance was guarded by a battery.

She shrugged while her mind began to narrow around a horrible idea. "At least no one was harmed," she stammered to Roseline's back as it departed. Emma's jaw tightened. The pirate known as Redbird sailed under an American flag. His swift ship, rumored to be named *Revenge*, robbed English and sometimes Spanish ships when it was convenient.

She stared at her reflection. Redbird had captured a Spanish trader nearby. Could he sneak into Pensacola? The man who'd startled her last night, threatened her, and almost kidnapped her had snuck up from behind. Who was he and why had he been sneaking along the shore? She stopped breathing and put a hand to her heart.

No, surely not. The pirate Redbird would not have let her go. The man last night had a kind, cultured voice even though he was stern. A pirate would have drowned her—or worse. She tucked a braid up behind her ear and made herself stand. Her attacker had behaved rather desperately when he realized she was not whomever he expected. He did not seem to recognize her, so she didn't have to worry Don Marcos might learn of her wanderings in the night that showed no appreciation for his protection and all he had done for her. She must never appear ungrateful.

Composed, Emma stepped into the hall. Around the corner to the don's wing of the house, she walked with proper, even steps as Roseline had shown her how to do. Here, Don Marcos kept his bedchambers, and across the hall, a narrow but long study filled with books and oil portraits and fine red and blue carpets. The windows were tall, much like the don, and let in light almost all of the day. It reflected off the white mineral-washed walls making the room glow perfectly for reading.

She entered at his gruff, *Entra,* and shut the door with a click behind her.

"Ah, good afternoon, my good daughter," he said in his native tongue.

Emma curtsied and stepped over to a velvet chair across from his ornate desk. She waited to be invited to sit. He lowered his chin, and she slipped down onto its softness. "Roseline said you wished to see me," she explained in halting Spanish.

Don Marcos appraised her with feathery brows. She'd never asked his age; his birthdays quietly came and went without notice although Roseline suggested he was well-near seventy.

"I hope you slept well despite the storm."

"Well enough," answered Emma. "

"Then we did not keep you up. There was unexpected business."

"Yes, I thought I heard someone. Is everything well?"

Don Marcos leaned back in his chair, and Emma waited for his explanation. He seemed to enjoy entrusting her with information of all kinds, a sort of faith that pleased her, but at the same time it reminded her that she was unimportant and who could she possibly tell?

He tapped his fingers on the desk next to a carved cigar box. "Yes, everything is as well as to be expected, but a ship was attacked on its way to Havana not long after departing the harbor yesterday."

"The *Revenge*?" wondered Emma although she already knew.

Surprise flickered in the don's eyes, and she hoped he was impressed. He was probably astounded that his noble daughter would know such things, but the truth was she was American and common. She regretted her guessing game.

"Sí," he replied in a cool tone. He flipped open the lid to his cigar box, and his fingers burrowed around. "The pirate Redbird is the reported villain. He did not kill the captain, but three men were wounded by cannon fire. The pirates had sharpshooters on the yardarms and nest, and they were armed with British pistols and cutlasses."

"They took only goods then?" urged Emma. "No one was harmed?"

"Yes, all of the hides and dried beef were stolen. I had a shipment aboard myself."

Emma frowned. "I'm sorry to hear this, Don Marcos." It made the story a little more personal now.

He ran his finger down the soft side of a cigar. "I had letters aboard. I sent an important missive to your older brother, you recall."

"Yes." Emma's stomach cringed. She did not know her brother, and after twenty-three years, she was sure her Spanish sibling had no interest in meeting Emma Rosa Montego, a child from her father's late season of life.

Don Marcos rearranged himself. His lack of enthusiasm to pontificate made Emma feel uneasy. She squeezed her fingers in her lap and waited patiently like Mrs. McKay—the only mother she'd ever known—had taught her to do.

She wondered if he'd loved her real mother at all. Certainly, her mama had been much younger than he. Had he seduced her? Had he broken her heart like in the gossip Betsy and the other servants exchanged over pots and laundry in the kitchen yard?

Don Marcos cleared his throat. When Emma returned her attention to him, a stiff, unnatural smile tugged his lips apart. "I have something exciting to tell you," he announced. Emma straightened. "We're going to have a birthday party."

Emma managed to stammer, "For who?"

"For you, my daughter," he answered as if she were silly. "Your birthday is in less than two weeks."

"I know." Emma tried to look pleased. That meant officials and merchants and all of their neighbors would come to whisper in Spanish and stare. The don did not do things small.

He turned the unlit cigar over in his fingers, and his eyes gleamed. "I will invite almost everyone in the settlement, and some from the fort and harbor, too."

Emma caught herself before her shoulders slumped. "Yes, Don Marcos, thank you."

He nodded, and she tried to brighten and collect herself. "Until then," he continued, "I must warn you to stay indoors and not go out to the courtyard without Roseline."

Emma stared in surprise. "Not even to the courtyard?"

The don shook his head as if it weighed a great deal. "You must not go out alone at all without one of us," he sighed. "Captain Redbird disappeared quickly. Too quickly." Don Marcos glanced out the window at the slanting of the sun. A vine of scarlet bougainvillea curled across the open shutter. "It is not safe for you to go out today, much less sit in the courtyard alone. The garrison is searching the outer islands."

"For Redbird?" Emma felt her forehead wrinkle, but her chest sank with suspicion.

"Indeed. He strikes to the east and the west of Pensacola, but never our port. Perhaps he is not escaping to the Indies as they say."

"You think he's close by?" Emma heard her voice raise in alarm. The memory of wading at the midnight shore, only to be shoved against a tree and nearly suffocated by a menacing shadow with a calm and courteous English voice made chills run down her back.

"Don't concern yourself, my child," said the don. He slanted his head and looked at her the way he admired his book collection. "I will ride out to the harbor later and make sure our little city in the sand is fiercely guarded. If the pirate Redbird is here, he won't be able to hide for long. We'll hunt him down, and he will be tried at Fort San Carlos de Barranca far from our little hacienda."

"Yes, Don Marcos." The rebuilding of the fort on the barrier island across the water was almost complete. It wasn't that far away. Emma rose to her feet and nearly forgot to curtsy. Her mind whirled like a flock of gulls. Had she nearly been kidnapped by the pirate Redbird?

CHAPTER TWO

Several miles due east of Pensacola Harbor on the fringes of a swampy mainland, Phillip watched the reassuring silhouette of his first mate on the *Revenge* cross the sand in confident strides. Chekilli, named after his honorable Creek ancestor, joined Phillip at the water's edge with nothing but a dagger on his hip. Without a word, they guided a small vessel upriver into the night and familiar tunnels of kingly oaks.

Phillip let out a heavy breath of relief. The day had been a success. The Montego lady had sounded no alarms, and he had made it safely to his little house in the settlement where he could make a pretense of innocence. His men could hide out in the shadows of the bayou, a choking, dank place closed off and hidden from the sea.

The pirogue glided up to the landing a few steps away from a camouflaged trail a band of Creeks used to come and go. Chekilli stepped out, and Phillip saw him make the sign for two days, and he returned it. Armed with Phillip's revelation about the girl at the shore, his friend ducked under the ghostly *barbe espagnol* moss and disappeared like an apparition.

Phillip continued paddling through the haunting swamp until the waterway split, and he was forced to heave his way through resting water until the pirogue scraped bottom. It sounded like a guttural growl in a silent night only perforated by whirring mosquitoes and flapping bats. He stepped into the shallows, making as small a splash as possible, and tugged the boat onto the bank where it would be camouflaged by knuckled mangroves. Struggling to find the trail without turning an ankle, he bullied his way through the trees until the foliage receded into a clearing.

Candlelight flickered between the boards and high windows of a shack. He hurried past outstretched branches, jerking in surprise when something brushed his shoulder. Jumping back, he went for his knife until he saw his assailant was a small key deer dangling upside down waiting to be gutted. Both disturbed and hungry, he stifled a chuckle under his breath.

He scrambled onto the raised porch that kept out alligators and snakes, and strode to the door not bothering to keep quiet should he alarm the swamp witch and find himself with a sharpened stick through his neck. Phillip rested a hand on the weathered board and in a raised tone, muttered the old Ashanti greeting she'd taught him. It creaked open, and as expected, she was swaying in her walnut rocking chair someone had traded her for a healing potion.

"Hello, Queenie Oba." He bowed like a proper Englishman, which he knew would amuse her coming from an American with no claims to great fortune or family. The red plumes in the band of his cocked hat and the scarlet sash around his hips worn aboard the *Revenge* bespoke what he truly was.

She pulled a smoldering clay pipe from her full lips. "I heard you coming from the mangrove swamp, pirate," she rebuked him. "It sounded like a bear crashing through my bayou." She waved him over with a faint smile. "Come, show me what Captain Redbird has brought his Queenie."

Phillip scraped his boots on a bristly rug then wound his way past casks of rice, rum, and a table littered with half-filled bottles of suspicious fluids. The open room smelled like cedar, dried flowers, and mouthwatering spices. He ducked to keep from slapping his head against the slanted roof and took a seat on a feather-tufted bench.

"Your ship is in my swamp."

"We won't be noticed," Phillip promised. "You can't see her keeled over and no one's about."

"Nobody is going to look for an ugly pirate in this shumpy old swamp anyway," Queenie agreed. A handsome, ebony-skinned woman with wide cheekbones, she didn't look a day older than he but for the silver streaks in her hair and the scars up her arms. The white of her eyes glimmered as bright as her teeth in a way he found mystical for a woman close to a century old.

"I brought you something." Her expectant grin widened, and Phillip reached into the leather bandolier slung across his chest and dug out the pocket watch. "From a very generous Spaniard," he grinned. He dangled it in the air by a short chain.

Queenie held out her small palm, and he set it in it. "It's rather new," he beamed, "and see that's gold trim on the back and the knob."

She held it up before her eyes and studied it.

"The Roman letters stand for numbers."

Queenie jerked her head back as if he'd said something ugly and dropped the timekeeper on her lap no longer interested. "I know how to tell time, Phillip-boy, I taught you."

He shifted on the bench when he saw her hand move to the clawed chicken foot hanging around her neck. She rolled it between her fingers, studying him. "You bring me a watch. I give you a warning."

Phillip stiffened. He didn't believe in the dark magic practiced in the West Indies, but he trusted Queenie. She was a vessel of knowledge—a woman of many worlds and generations.

He forced a chuckle. "You didn't have another dream, did you? Were you mixing the *cassina* and rum again?" He winked, and she hooked a finger at him.

"I don't mix my black tea with that poison when I have the best honey."

"And a yearling out there that needs attention."

"Yes," she agreed, still pinching the chicken foot. "You take care of that deer before you go."

He dipped his chin. "Yes, ma'am." Phillip hoped that would appease her, but Queenie kept staring at him with sparkling eyes that hinted at a secret. There was no ignoring it or pretending to forget it. She never forgot anything—nothing she saw, heard, or read.

"We overtook a Spanish merchantman," he admitted. "I couldn't resist."

She wagged her head. "To feed folk like me? Or to make them pay for your family's deaths?"

Her blunt question felt like a punch to the chest. Phillip rarely talked about his brother or his parents. "It's my life's work," he said with a shrug, looking around the cabin at the bouquets of brown, shriveled herbs, "much like yours. I help other people by taking payment from those who owe me."

"Mmm," she grunted. "I know the British shot your brother while the Spanish stood by, but you can't satisfy your pain with theft and money."

Phillip looked at the swept floorboards. "I know, Queenie, but why sit in a great house in Jamaica with more than I will ever need and do nothing to avenge them."

She raised her wiry brows in disdain. "You have a fleet of fishing boats and that great merchantman named after your mama. Why do you need a pirate ship, too?"

He shrugged. "If I'm going to sail between Louisiana and Havana, not to mention cruise into Pensacola to fill my coffers, why not make the English as miserable as they made me? No one suspects I abandon the *Mary Alice* at sea to sneak aboard and sail the *Revenge*."

Queenie made a snorting noise. "Those who hunt trouble find tragedy," she warned. She raised the chicken foot so he could see it. "I dreamed a dream, Phillip-boy, and tossed the bones."

Phillip sighed as a ripple of concern traveled down his back, but this was a part of their ritual whenever he visited her. "What did you see?" She would not tell if he did not ask.

"I saw the sun going down fast, and heard the dark night growling like a wildcat.

He studied her gnarled hand so different from her ageless face. "I'm running out of time?"

She inclined her chin. "Trouble is brewing for you and your buccaneers."

Phillip stared at the floor instead of the smelly candles that dripped wax-like tears. Which ship? he wondered. The *Mary Alice*—his merchantman that sailed a triangular route between West Florida and the Caribbean? Or the *Revenge*? His sleek and speedy schooner with shining cannonades that could overtake a heavily-laden trader moving goods back to England.

Phillip knew Queenie didn't approve of his attacks on British ships in the *Revenge*, but it was well-deserved justice. Besides, it wasn't like he involved the *Mary Alice* or any of his other legal businesses. "They kidnapped me, burned my home, murdered my parents, and shot my brother at sea. England took everything that ever mattered away from me," muttered Phillip. "Spain may have supported our cause during the revolution, but when David's ship was attacked, they did nothing. Maybe he could have swum to St. Augustine if he'd survived."

A mournful owl gave a long, low hoot outside the window, and Phillip flinched. He looked at Queenie with derision on his face. "There's your second witness," she pointed out. "You can't live for revenge the rest of your life, boy, or your life will be cut short before you see nine and twenty." She glanced toward an hourglass poised on her long boarded table dripping specks of sand. "Hate will eat holes in you, and you'll sink like one of your boats," she predicted.

Phillip lifted his shoulders in some semblance of agreement. "I understand, and thank you for your concern." He allowed a cutting laugh. "It's not like anyone else cares if I sink or swim." Her clamped lips showed she was not happy with his reply. He glanced at the table. "I don't suppose you have anything better to eat than love potions or dried seaweed, do you?"

Queenie beamed at once, her irritation dismissed. She always had fat frog legs waiting for her Phillip-boy.

THE HUNT FOR PIRATES lurking around Pensacola and the outlying Creek lands commenced. Emma sat and embroidered beside Roseline in the drawing room, while they observed visitors come and go in a flurry of patriotic hunger to protect their Spanish frontier.

Pensacola was a stew of men, women, and children with mixed bloodlines much like Emma. North of the settlement squatted rows of platform cabins where many of the free Creoles lived. Some of them, she could tell, had European features much like hers, but no one spoke about that. Her Irish mamma's blood had lightened her skin, but her hair shined as dark and rich as the don's, her one saving grace among her wary neighbors who had finally come to accept her as her Spanish and manners improved.

Excitement tumbled up the street toward the edges of the settlement where row houses rested and the gardens grew. Several groups of soldiers and men galloped past the house until Emma could stand it no longer. She urged Roseline to her feet and outside to the courtyard. Standing against the rails of iron grating allowed a peek into the street.

"I suppose if there are pirates in the settlement they will be found," Roseline mused.

Emma made a small noise of agreement. She hoped so. She was rather curious as to where Captain Redbird had disappeared and found herself studying the gentlemen who came in and out of the house while worrying about the man who'd interrupted her beach walk.

"Here comes Señor Hidalgo," murmured Roseline under her breath.

A group of men on horseback ambled by in much less hurry than the guard. Their cocked hats were slanted low against the sun as they spoke in quiet tones to one another. One of the men looked up and saw her and brought his mount to a halt. He removed his hat.

"Señoritas," he called with a sharp grin from beneath his mustache.

Emma lifted her chin and Roseline replied, "Señor Hidalgo. You are off on an adventure, I see."

"Yes," he admitted, and one of his friends swept off his hat, too. "Señor Baca and Mr. Oakley are accompanying me out with the guard to sweep the pastures and surrounding forest." He made it sound like he was leading the entire expedition.

"For the pirate, I assume?" queried Roseline.

"Ah, yes," Señor Hidalgo explained, then he proceeded to reiterate the events at sea earlier in the week. The men looked rather excited, all but for one.

Emma studied Señor Hidalgo's friend who hung back. He was not Spanish and looked rather bored, his gaze shifting around the hacienda and up the street. Tall and broad-shouldered, he was a strapping man with a handsome square chin. Emma narrowed her eyes. There were not that many people like her in Pensacola, and he looked familiar.

His snapping blue gaze swept along the grounds of the hacienda and over the courtyard wall. When it met Emma's stare, the force of their connection made her step back. His horse stamped and whirled as if he'd dug in his heels and jerked the reins. She drew in a breath. The gentleman bowed his head, disinterested now, but he was too late, because Emma had felt an inquisitive hunger in the brief flash of his glance. Such eyes. As blue as a bluebird. He mumbled something to his companions, and they agreed.

"Good morning, then," called the two, and Roseline waved her handkerchief. Emma plastered a smile on her face. "Good luck, Mr. Oakley," called Roseline. He looked back briefly and touched the brim of his hat at them both. This time he stared directly at Emma's companion as if Emma was invisible. It didn't matter, but it made her smart for some reason. She waited until their backs became small in the distance.

"Who was that?"

"Who?" wondered Roseline with a turn of her head.

Emma lifted her shoulders as if it was not important. She did not want to seem too interested, but she could not stop herself from asking, "The quiet man in the back. Mr. Oakley?"

"The American," explained Roseline turning to the shade in the courtyard. She took Emma by the elbow and guided her out of the sun. "He has met once or twice with the don in the past, I believe, although it has been some time."

"He's a merchant?" Emma thought she knew all of the merchants in Pensacola.

"He owns the *Mary Alice*, you remember."

Emma shook her head.

"I only see him three or four times a year," guessed Roseline, "not that I take note of all of the comings and goings."

Emma made a noise of agreement but said under her breath, "Well, he does stand out I must say."

"Yes, I suppose," agreed her friend. "It's good of him to assist the señors with the search."

Emma ducked under the cool branches of a ripening orange tree. "Yes," she murmured, her mind stretching for something she could not see, "quite good of him indeed."

ALTHOUGH HE WAS NOT a soldier, Phillip joined a small search party, mostly merchants, miners, and fishermen, frightened of the thought of a pirate in their waters. He almost regretted it when he came across Miss Montego standing at her courtyard wall. The worst thing that could happen would be for her to recognize him, and foolishly, he'd tried to get a good look of her in the daylight and caught her eye.

My, how handsome she'd grown. Even more so if it were possible. Recalling her little waist when he'd scooped her up in his arms and the feel of her breath against his hand made him flinch hard enough to startle his poor horse. Had she noticed? He hoped not. Luckily, his companions had been too overcome with the excitement over their first and hopefully last ever pirate hunt to notice.

They'd scouted the land around the fort as far as their boundaries with the Creek. He supposed the governor might think a pirate would have a treaty that superseded Spain's understanding with the indigenous people, and he would be right. So, on his borrowed horse, Phillip joined the intrepid avengers tromping through the brush to as far as the swampy bayou. There they stopped. No one was interested in looking further into an alligator and wildcat-infested bog for lurkers. It was as Phillip hoped, and he found himself feeling more confident and safe as they made their way back home in the late afternoon.

The lieutenant-governor had planned a dinner party in his fine brick home for the holiday. He and his officials decided the festivities for the Feast of San Juan Bautista would go on as planned, and they would celebrate the summer solstice despite the pirate attack. A swell of excitement bobbed around the settlement, especially among the few young women and wives of the officers, because a bonfire would be lit at the beach which meant at some point dancing and revelry would commence.

As the settlement planned to celebrate, pirate or not, Phillip intended to attend. He'd worked hard to climb the ranks of social order, first as a boy and prisoner, then as a fisherman and eventual trader and merchant. But first, he sent a message with the results of the clumsy pirate hunt to Chekilli through one of the local trader's servants. His half-Creek and half-Spanish friend had worked at his side since his arrival to Pensacola as a boy with the British. He commandeered the crew of the *Revenge* when Phillip was putting on airs with officials in the ports and so he needed to be on the alert for pirate hunters in the swamp.

Afterward, he put on his finest white shirt and waistcoat. Despite his income, he insisted he could dress himself and did not hire out. It was hot for another layer, but he wore his bright blue coat set aside for special occasions. Before he departed, he took one last cautious look in the looking glass to check his hair. A tinted wax kept it clean and proper and disguised the rusty locks that looked quite red in the sun. It was silly to streak it with scarlet paint whenever he took over greedy Englishmen's ships, but it secretly amused him and the crew.

He smiled to himself as the widow's nag was brought around. There was no need for a carriage, heaven knew he didn't need one, so he cantered south along the smoothed street to the governor's home for dinner. Phillip was anxious to

see if the hysteria over the *Revenge* had calmed, and he wondered if the daughter of Don Marcos would attend.

She should not have recognized him in the darkness. With
his hat pulled low and dressed in simple attire, it would have
been too difficult to make out who he was in the dim night.
He wouldn't have been assured of her true identity himself if he
hadn't seen her pass by the glowing torch in the courtyard. His
concern now was whether or not she'd reported him and if the
officials had put two and two together. Surely the news would
have spread like wildfire, but he had heard nothing.

The lieutenant-governor and his frail wife greeted him in
a tastefully furnished drawing room. After paying his respects,
Phillip joined the other merchants of his class and mingled in
the corners until dinner. He waited restlessly for Don Marcos
to appear, and when he did, the young woman at his side nearly
swept Phillip's breath away.

"You decided to join us after all," welcomed Señor Hidalgo,
who'd snuck up beside him. The merchant, who exchanged
silks and other luxuries between Louisiana and Havana, leaned
closer to capture Phillip's attention when the don walked into
the room. "A fine feather for one's cap, the Señorita Montego,"
he furthered in a murmur.

Phillip raised a brow in agreement. "It's been some time
since I was introduced," he replied in a low tone, "although I
have exchanged bows with her papa."

He had seen Miss Montego at dinners and celebrations before, and occasionally from the distance in her fine carriage.
Why did she make his blood race now? Her hair was a rich
polished wood color and streaked with gold and copper from
the grueling Florida sun. It set off her peach blossom skin and

framed her dark eyes. Curious eyes. Watchful eyes. The near-ebony eyes of her papa no matter who her fair mama had been. She looked like a Spanish doll in her gold damask and tiny pearl-encrusted bodice. Her eyes swept the room, and Phillip averted his gaze lest he reveal all his secrets with his gawking examination.

"Her papa's final and enduring joy," murmured Phillip. Beside him, Hidalgo continued to admire her, too. He cocked his head. "I understand her father is growing anxious for a match."

"Indeed?" Phillip couldn't resist another examination of the Spanish jewel. "I assumed he would want her for himself to care for him in his old age."

"And old he is," agreed Hidalgo. "He's lucky to have a woman here to fetch his drink even if she is a daughter."

"He's been widowed twice I understand." Phillip turned to a window. His companion angled himself slightly as well. "Thrice," Hidalgo corrected him, "as Señorita Montego evidences."

Phillip raised his chin in acknowledgment. Hidalgo had not mentioned any rumors that the lovely Miss Montego had been accosted in the night. Phillip had been correct in suspecting she would not want anyone to know she was out of bed.

The bell rang for dinner, and he waited for his superiors to march from the room with their wives on their arms. He followed behind Hidalgo, one of the last to leave, but took a seat at the long table not sorry to be dining on heaps of fish and oysters followed by haunches of venison and the don's fine beef.

Phillip carried on politely with the other merchants and mine owners around him. Sneaking a glance down the table at Miss Montego on occasion, he noted an officer in crisp naval dress. Gold and scarlet cuffs gleamed from his coat. "Who is that?" he wondered in a low tone to Hidalgo.

The merchant looked at him in wide-eyed surprise. He grinned, showing the gap between his upper teeth. "You did not know? The hunter, *León,* arrived just hours ago."

"A *guardacosta*?"

"Sí. She's rather heavy for it, but too small to do any real damage to a bigger ship of the line."

Phillip looked down at his plate to disguise his alarm. How had he missed the news a *guardacosta* had arrived? He felt Hidalgo studying him. "The *Mary Alice* did not stay long after I disembarked," he explained, "she sailed out this afternoon. I have business here, and she has trade in Louisiana."

"Ah, I see." Hidalgo accepted the explanation. "You trust your captain. Captain Page, is it?"

"Completely," breathed Phillip. Concerned, he forced himself to listen without gazing at the guests at the other end of the table. However, when dessert was served, he found it impossible not to take a sweeping look around the room again. The Spanish captain appeared focused on Don Marcos. Miss Montego bent over her plate with downcast eyes.

She had matured. Something about her carriage and character seemed to have stepped forward out of the timid shadows. True, it had been months since his ships had sailed into Pensacola waters, but how had he not noticed? Perhaps he'd been too busy focusing on what was within reach. He was a different man than when he'd first arrived in West Florida as a boy on a British gunship, and he'd never assumed himself worthy of a nobleman's daughter. Dare he now?

Phillip watched Miss Montego take a dainty sip with her little mouth. Something curious stirred in his chest. She looked his direction, and he dropped his stare with a pounding heart. How much did she know about him? Her gaze had been curious when she'd met his examination earlier in the street. His pulse quickened. Perhaps she did suspect something, but how to find out...

CHAPTER THREE

The sky glowed lavender as the heat of the day dissipated in cool breezes wafting across the water. Emma studied the distant lights glowing from the small battery being rebuilt on the island across from the harbor. If one didn't know the difference, they'd think the glimmers were stars dotting the darkening horizon.

The bonfire was lit as dinner settled in Emma's stomach. Around her, the crowd of revelers grew as those who had not been invited to dinner arrived for the festivities on the shore. It was a variety of humanity that included soldiers, officers, merchants, shopkeepers, farmers, fishermen, and even miners; all with partners on their arms and anxious to dance. It looked like everyone in Pensacola would celebrate tonight.

She wondered if the man she'd met on the shore the night before lurked nearby and moved closer to Don Marcos's side. Examining the guests, she kept her gaze averted from the Spanish captain who'd stared at her through dinner as if she was on the menu. She wished Roseline had come. Emma frowned as the growing flames of the bonfire licked up the tall pyramid of logs. Soon, the fire would touch the sky and glowing embers would dance around in the breeze like sprites. How she wanted to dance.

Dancing would be difficult. She glanced down at her new gown. There were only two seamstresses in Pensacola, so she and Roseline had done much of the work. It was a stunning piece, so different from the rough wool dresses pulled over her head when she was a child in the McKay's modest home. She picked up a heavy pleat and rubbed it between her fingers. As hot as she'd felt during dinner, it was cooler now, and she tried to relax as a cool breeze whipped across her neck and ruffled her hem. Would she ever get used to being a nobleman's daughter?

The smell of celebratory drink drifted through the air over the scent of crackling wood. Restless, she whispered to Don Marcos, "I'm going to step down to the beach closer to the water."

"Are you too warm?"

"Not too much," she assured him.

"But you should dance."

"Oh, I..." Emma glanced around. She was seldom asked. Young men her age were too intimidated, and the don's friends were married or old. Her chest tightened. She glanced up at her father to show her hesitation.

"Don't wander too far," said the don, and he patted her hand and released it. Emma watched him make a beeline for the lieutenant governor and his wife. A row of good chairs had been dragged outside without any concern that they would be marred by salt and heat. There the officials would lord over the crowd.

Emma plastered a smile on her face as couples around her began clapping and laughing. She edged away toward the quieter shoreline where thinning waves receded from the shore.

The moon had finally overtaken the sky as the sun surrendered its longest reign of the year. She looked out across the violet sea and breathed in the peace it offered.

"*Buenas noches*," said a quiet voice from behind her.

Emma swept her chin over her shoulder. Her new companion stepped up beside her, and she inched away to get a better look at him in the bonfire light. It was not Captain Gonzalez she discovered with some relief. "Hello," returned Emma in a breathless voice. "Señor—"

"Oakley," he reminded her. "Mr. Phillip Oakley. I have shipped for your father on the rare occasion."

The merchant at her courtyard, yes, and he was an American. She found herself allowing a brief curtsy although she owed him none. "Yes, I recall," she responded with politeness.

"You are not enjoying the bonfire?" His deep voice sent a tremor down her spine. She recognized it somehow.

"It's warm," she stammered. He watched her closely, and her heart began to stumble along in a queer way.

"Yes, the flames are bright enough to see for leagues. Even the battery would not be needed if we were in want of a beacon tonight."

Emma tried to look agreeable although something about him made her feel peculiar. Why did Mr. Oakley wish to speak with her? There was something meaningful in the way he examined her face.

"We are lucky," he continued. "It was not this bright last night or the night before. With the cloud cover, one could barely see his hand in front of his face at times."

A sliver of warning snaked through Emma's mind. The night before last? Her heart hesitated. In stature, he was a close match to the shadow of the man who'd accosted her. He spoke perfect English, with a slight American accent that raised the little hairs on the back of her neck. "I suppose," she managed to reply in a tight voice. It was too dark to examine him any closer, but she'd noted him in the drawing room before dinner. Besides toasted, tawny skin and distracting blue eyes, she'd admired his shining short locks. They were more auburn than brown. Why, in the bright sun, they would be as good as red...

Emma's heart leaped over a beat. As if in agreement, a flash of light from the bonfire lit his face. Three little scratches were clustered on the top of his cheek. Her mind flashed back to the shadow she'd grappled with in the dark. She had clawed a face. Hadn't she? Emma felt her breath *whoosh* out of her. "Good evening," she gulped and turned to flee. Had she just met her assailant? If so, what had Mr. Oakley been doing on the shore in the middle of the night? Why had he pushed her against a tree and smothered her cries with his rough hand? And just what had he intended to do with her when he'd snatched her from the water?

Emma made it to the edges of the dancing and tried to camouflage her alarm. She searched the crowd for Don Marcos. Dare she mention it? She wrung her hands. Perhaps she was wrong. She could easily be mistaken. She drew in a shaky breath to calm herself. She'd slept poorly and had felt jumpy all afternoon. It was quite late now. Perhaps her imagination had run away with her. The American just gave her confused feelings.

Through the crowd, her eyes met the curious gaze of Captain Gonzalez, and her nerves tangled in her throat. Perhaps it would not be a bad idea if he asked her to dance. Beside her, someone took her elbow, and she looked up at Don Marcos, but it was not him. It was Mr. Oakley again.

"Señorita," he murmured with an odd expression. "Let us dance." Without waiting for her consent, Mr. Oakley pulled her into the throng of dancers twirling around the giant blaze like pagans. There was too much fun for anyone to notice her unease.

Mr. Oakley spun Emma about in dizzying circles with his hand clasped tightly around her fingers. His eyes were locked on hers like a bird of prey. Emma's heart thundered with exertion and apprehension. She could hardly catch her breath in her squeezing stays. Her wide heavy skirts swung around her legs like rugs and threatened to make her stumble.

She watched a blur of faces go by and tried to decide whether or not to pull away and hurry over to Don Marcos. It would be rude, but who would notice? Don Marcos, the lieutenant-governor, and their friends chatted and laughed like everyone else in the crushing swarm. It was as if all of West Florida danced under the moon tonight. Was there anyone left in town?

She stumbled, and her knees gave way. Mr. Oakley caught her by the elbows, and before she knew it, guided her away from the bonfire toward the dark shore.

"Sir," Emma said with a rush of hot fear searing her bones, "I cannot take a turn without a chaperone." Where was Roseline? she wondered. Had she come? She'd said she would be along in the evening.

"We are not going out too far," soothed Mr. Oakley in a congenial tone. "See, the party is just behind us, and look, the moon is lighting up the heavens, and the trees are glowing."

Emma didn't see anything glowing. She swept a look over her shoulder toward the party and saw it shrinking in the distance. Whether or not he was just flirting or the actual guilty party of her scare on the beach, this would not do. She reminded herself who she was now. "Mr. Oakley," she declared with bravado, "I will not go any further. If you wish to converse, we must do so by the light of the bonfire."

"How about beneath a tree?" came the smooth retort.

Emma looked up at her escort in surprise. Was he confessing?

"I know there is no one about but did you know," wondered Mr. Oakley, holding her firmly as he set a course for a cluster of palms, "there is a path beyond the grove here that winds around the back of the settlement. They use it at the fort for guard duty and such. I understand it goes as far as the Creek's borders."

She knew his meaning and was certain this was the man who'd acted torn between embracing her or harming her only a night ago. Emma jerked away, but he moved between her and the bonfire. "And there are tributaries that run into the bayous," she finished. She locked her knees. She was not some helpless, ignorant, or spoiled heiress. She'd run the streets of Charleston and practically raised Mrs. McKay's rowdy little boys in the swampy low country. Not to mention, she had not fallen to pieces at the startling revelation she was a don's daughter and would be dragged across the ocean to a sweltering, sandy strip of Florida frontier. Emma made fists with her trembling hands.

Mr. Oakley's eyes glittered in the moonlight. "Indeed. You know a great deal about Pensacola."

She didn't wait for him to threaten her any further. "If you are implying, sir, that we have encountered one another on your little path, then I'm sure I don't know what you mean." She hoped he would simply forget it.

"If we have," volleyed Mr. Oakley, in a voice changed from charming to chilling, "than I am sure you will not mention it. To anyone."

Emma forced herself not to visibly shiver. "I will mention it to anyone I see fit," she retorted.

His handsome, rugged face became menacing. "My business is my own," he uttered in a threatening tone, "and I see no reason for you to mention we bumped into one another outside your courtyard." He hesitated, and before Emma could respond, added, "unless you wish me to tell your father we rendezvous often along the midnight shore and with you in your nightdress."

Her mouth gaped at his implications. "How dare you even suggest such a thing. I am not that sort."

"Perhaps," he rasped in a more confident tone, "but who would not believe it when all of Pensacola wonders why the pretty Señorita Montego has not yet wed?"

Emma squeezed her fingers as her cheeks flamed. "Because there is no one who prefers me over Don Marcos!" She wondered at once why she said it. Mr. Oakley did not need to know she understood that any man who condescended to marry her was only interested in the don's power and wealth, not a half-Spaniard woman. She choked down the fear pooling in her throat. "Why I am unwed is none of your affair, and you have no right skulking along the shore frightening anyone out for a walk."

"I thought you were in trouble," Mr. Oakley explained in a dry tone, "but perhaps you had a clandestine meeting with another gentleman."

"You are hardly a gentleman," Emma snapped. "I was trying to find seashells. It was hot—"

"In the dark? All alone?"

"Most people sleep at night," she retorted. "Except for—"

"Except for naughty señoritas who sneak out of their courtyards."

"I was not going to meet anyone!" she hissed. "I like the sea, and I know how to swim." How could this man make her as angry as Mrs. McKay's impish boys? She'd behaved as reserved and proper as she knew how since arriving in Pensacola, and Roseline had taught her even more, but Mr. Oakley made her want to revert back to the self she hid inside.

The corners of his mouth turned up, and Emma huffed. "Mr. Oakley," she sniffed, "keep your secrets. I will not tell anyone you attacked me on the seashore, and you will not tell anyone you saw me there."

"In your nightdress," he amended with a roguish grin.

"My dressing gown." Was he a gentleman or not? Emma squared her shoulders. "Do we have a bargain then?"

He stuck out his hand, and she stared in distaste. "Shake my hand like a good American, *Miss* Montego, and we have a deal."

"I'm not – I'm – fine!" Emma offered her hand, and he swallowed it with a bear-sized paw then gave it a gentle wiggle. It was ludicrous, considering he was blackmailing her for such a little thing.

Satisfied, Mr. Oakley turned and examined the party in the distance.

"Tell me, Mr. Oakley," Emma wondered aloud, "what were *you* doing wading along the shore? You are not a part of the night watch."

Mr. Oakley looked back at her with penetrating eyes then offered an arm to escort her to the bonfire. "Don't you worry your pretty little head about it, Miss Montego. The less you know, the better." He met her stare with a warning look. She shifted her gaze to the short burnished locks sweeping across the top of his forehead. Light from the fire shined off them turning them scarlet-red. As red as a redbird.

THE DAYS FOLLOWING the summer solstice felt as if Mother Nature wanted to stoke the fires of summer herself. Phillip stayed in Saturday and played cards with Chekilli. His friend was ignored by the Spaniards due to his history with the pelt traders at the frontier's crossroads where he and Phillip had struck up a brotherhood so many years ago.

They gambled until it was cool enough to walk to the harbor and surreptitiously counted the naval vessels and one small privateer. Phillip took especial note of the large *guardacosta* dispatched from Havana. Chekilli whispered in Creek that it had a young and ambitious captain named Gonzalez.

Phillip recalled Gonzalez from the lieutenant-governor's party. The captain had small watchful eyes. He looked much like a clever raptor and that meant staying out of sight and mind of the commander. Phillip tensed as they walked past a group of officers from the *León* and forced himself to mimic

Chekilli's easy gait past a boisterous tavern spilling its sailors and soldiers into the street.

They ambled on to a more suitable establishment for the merchant class, and heads turned to examine the newly-arrived American and native when they entered. Strangers were not unwelcome here, as long as they paid the tariffs without complaint and caused no trouble. Phillip raised a hand in greeting at two merchants he'd dealt with a few times. Spotting Señor Hidalgo, he drifted toward his table and party. Phillip bowed, and they invited him to sit. He pulled out a chair for Chekilli, ignoring their slight.

"You are still with us," said Hidalgo with a wide grin beneath his thick mustache.

Phillip lifted his shoulders in a half-shrug. "I sent the *Mary Alice* onto Louisiana so I could tend to matters here, you recall. I do not mind the view and breezes. It's so much nicer than a squalid city."

The others nodded in agreement. "I think it's clever of you," declared Señor Baca. "Why let her sit in the harbor like a lazy wench when her captain can finish your route while you do business here?"

Phillip smiled at his approval. "I have exchanges to make at the treasury, what with all this muddle of currency, and my man and I have a shipment of pelts we expect to arrive anytime from the territory."

Another gentleman picked up a bottle of drink and sniffed it. "You've had great success trading for pelts with the Creeks, I hear." He did not bother to acknowledge Chekilli.

"I've dwelt in Pensacola here and there in my life. It was an opportune time to make trusted connections before the treaty removed the Redcoats."

"You trade in Havana from time to time?"

Phillip avoided the Spanish capital as much as possible. "Most of my business is among the other islands," he divulged, hoping to drive their minds away from any plunderers along the coast, "as is my home, too. I see no reason not to share the bounty of the West Indies with my West Florida friends."

Hidalgo held up his glass. "Smart man."

The other man looked confused. "But you are American."

"I was a British prize, one might say," Phillip explained, "during the war. When it ended, I chose to stay in the Indies."

"Ah." The men seemed satisfied.

Baca motioned toward him. "We don't trust all the Americans lurking around the territory. They make friends with the Creeks and turn them against us."

"You'll have no problem here," Phillip assured them. "The bands nearby do not like them or their ideas of expansion."

"So you were a turncoat then?" prodded someone else.

Phillip gave a tight smile to show it took great effort to reign in his annoyance at the impertinent question. "I was not. The British killed my family, burned my home to the ground, and forced me onto one of their gunships."

"I'm sorry," came the reply.

Baca patted the man on the back. "He means no offense, Señor Oakley. He is only frustrated and angry at this American pirate."

"Oh?" Phillip raised a brow.

"I lost a great deal of income," admitted the man. "All that work gone to waste," he complained. "I sent my oranges to Havana aboard Peña's ship, you see, and now they are gone. I will need to find a loan."

Phillip tried not to grin. He was glad he'd eaten a few of the señor's oranges, as he clearly had not bothered to grow them himself. Phillip had no pity for enslavers who lost what they had not rightfully earned in the forests and fruit orchards.

"What of this pirate?" he wondered, trying to act stupid. "I've only heard of him on the rare occasion. He's never troubled my ship."

"Yes, well," argued Hidalgo in broken English, "the *Mary Alice* is not a big ship."

Phillip shrugged. "Or heavy. I keep my trade route small, and as you see, don't let her waste time in port, even if I do." He took a swallow of good wine.

"And when will she return?"

Phillip did not want to give such information away so he tried to look suspicious. "I never share my schedules, Señor Baca," he chided, "that would be dangerous."

"Especially with Captain Redbird about," agreed Hidalgo. He raised a hairy fist. "It won't be long before he's captured," he predicted in a threatening hiss, "for we have the *León* from the *Armada Española* guarding our waters now."

"Mmm," grunted Phillip as if impressed. Actually, it was a concern. The *León* was a ship of the line—granted a small one converted for a *guardacosta's* mission—but he estimated she carried twenty-six cannons to his sixteen. "Then perhaps our worries are irrelevant," Phillip suggested.

But his stomach clenched. He fought the burning urge to run back to the bayou, set the *Revenge* to rights, and set sail for Jamaica straight away. Unfortunately, he could not leave the *Mary Alice* uninformed as to his whereabouts. He'd have to sit and wait it out. The delivery of his pelts was impending anyway, although he'd happily float them through the bayou to the pirate ship and avoid the taxes.

"Well, gentlemen," Phillip declared with pretended regret, "I must bid you a good night before the guard comes around and throws us all out."

Baca nodded. "You will be at the don's this Saturday next? For the party?"

"My, another party." Phillip hesitated. The governor's invitation had been a rare and welcome surprise albeit it was a special occasion. He'd received no invite from the don.

"Yes," continued Baca, "his daughter's birthday. Rarely does he celebrate anything in private, you must know. He has no wife, no *familia*, except for this young woman he brought from the American colonies."

"She is a proper lady, though," intervened Hidalgo.

"Loyal to the crown, I am sure," Phillip agreed with a forced smile. His chest tightened. Could he trust her? Was it safe to stay in Pensacola when only one whisper from a respected and observant young lady could send officers and officials to investigate him more closely? He leaned over to Baca and tried to sound curious rather than eager. "How does one procure an invitation to such a party as this?"

Baca smiled. "I suppose one must be wealthy or an unmarried man. Perhaps you should come on my arm, Señor Oakley."

The men around the table cracked into shards of laughter. Phillip sat back as if amused. "Of course, Señor Baca," he agreed as if doing him a favor, "I would be happy to accompany you and keep you entertained."

EMMA FELT CLOSE TO ill carrying around her secret that a man had attacked her on her midnight walk and then blackmailed her into silence. Glancing up from her embroidery, she scanned the trees and cactus behind the courtyard fence as if Mr. Oakley was spying on her from there.

"What are you looking for, my dear?"

"Oh! Roseline. I did not see you come out." Emma made herself chuckle and hoped she didn't sound uneasy.

"I brought your lime and water. It's good water from the spring."

Emma accepted it with an appreciative smile. "I still find it odd to have a fine home and lovely courtyard here while the garden that feeds our household and everyone else's is north of the settlement."

Roseline shrugged. "It's easier that way, and Betsy finds it convenient to trade when short on a melon or in excess of vegetables."

"I suppose," decided Emma, and then she went on to tell Roseline about the marketplace in Charleston and all of the shops and inns around the wharves. Betsy came out of the hacienda just as it was beginning to feel too warm to stay outside.

"Don Marcos has called for the carriage," she announced, and Emma passed her sewing over to Roseline with a discreet sigh. At least all of their talk had distracted her from Mr. Oakley, whose nefarious deeds had kept her awake the past few nights. She'd never had a secret, not a dangerous one, and it puzzled her as to what to do with it. She could not imagine the expression on Roseline's face if she were to learn her meek, obedient ward traipsed down to the seaside to pick up shells, caress sea turtles, and study the moon like a wild child with no proper training.

"I should go up," Emma murmured.

"Don't forget your shawl," Roseline reminded her as she walked toward the house.

Emma had agreed to ride with Don Marcos to the treasury, and she often did so about once a week. She enjoyed the jaunt around town in his exquisite carriage. The McKays never had anything like it except for a wobbly wagon. He was waiting in the open carriage under its sunshade when Emma passed through the door with a parasol in her gloved hands. In truth, she'd rather have a little time in the sun's rays to deepen her skin like everyone else's, but the don insisted she stay creamy and fair. His assistant, a secretary they called Pablo, hurried by in a ruffle of papers. His jaw was clamped shut, and a sheen of perspiration shined across his forehead. The don had little patience for inefficiency.

Trying her best to look as though she'd been summoned from a busy morning rather than the gated courtyard, Emma stepped gracefully into the carriage and dropped beside him. He liked her to share the same view or perhaps he preferred her undivided attention.

"Good morning," he murmured as he reclined into the cushion behind his back. Emma rearranged her layers. "Good morning, Don Marcos," she returned in Spanish. She squinted into the blinding white sun. "There are no clouds today. Perhaps we will skip our daily rain shower."

He smiled at her. "One never knows. I've come to learn if I don't care for the weather at the moment, I only need to wait it out. It's never the same from one hour to the next."

Emma gave an agreeable nod and laid the parasol across her lap as the driver snapped the whip. The don's two gleaming horses jerked forward like they wanted to run away. He made a noise of irritation at being jolted in his seat.

"I have finished my last pillow," blurted Emma after straining for a suitable bit of banter that would not bore him to death.

"I'm sure it's lovely," he murmured confirming her worst fears.

Why did he pretend to like her company cantering up and down the streets of Pensacola with him? It was not that she minded her view from the fine carriage, seeing her neighbors, or observing the activity along the fort and in the harbor, but she did seem to weary him so. "Will you be long in the treasury today?" There was a new dry goods shop near the heart of the settlement, and Emma ached to see it but knew not how to ask.

"I promise to be quick," he assured her. "You will accompany me inside?"

"I dislike to trouble you."

"You don't trouble me at all. I find I'm given better attention when I have a lady at my side." Emma felt her mouth fall, and a soft laugh of disbelief escaped. "It's just as well," added the don, "for I wanted to speak with you about your birthday."

Her face warmed knowing that enormous attention would be heaped upon her at her birthday dinner. She dreaded all of it, for no one who said anything kind to her could mean it. They were the don's friends and connections, not hers. Only a few of the wives spoke to her at all, and it was usually nothing beyond gowns or her coiffure—also her father's creations in a manner of speaking, for Roseline needed his approval for every little thing.

"You are too kind to me," Emma murmured, but the muscles in her back tightened. He was kind in his own way, but she didn't understand him and doubted any of it was heartfelt. She was a duty. His duty.

"I'd hoped to make an announcement at your party," he confided, "but my letters to Spain were interrupted by this Captain Redbird."

At the mention of the pirate Redbird, Emma fell quiet. Did the curious Mr. Oakley have something to do with it after all? He was certainly secretive when he was not humiliating her with threats that he would tell the don her secrets.

"I see you are troubled," the don observed. He patted her arm. "Don't be. With Captain Gonzalez here, all will soon be under control."

"I'm not afraid, Don Marcos." Emma pulled back her shoulders. "No one can take Pensacola harbor anyway. Like you say, it's too deep and well-protected."

He smiled, pleased to hear her echo his own words. "It is, and though we are the unofficial capital of West Florida," he boasted, "we are still a settlement here. Things could change at any time, and I must keep you safe."

Emma looked at him with a tingle of curiosity. "Is there something I should know?"

His lips stretched into something like a very-near smile. "Dear Emma," he said, "I have decided it would be best if you were sent home to Spain."

Home? He made it sound like he'd bequeathed her a castle, but Emma's heart turned to marble in her chest, a stone so heavy she could not breathe. The horizon began to spin.

"Now, don't be alarmed. I feel the time is past due. Since my assignment here is not complete, I will stay, but after all these years I feel you must meet your brother so you have someone when I am gone."

The only family Emma had ever known were Mr. and Mrs. McKay and their mischievous children. They'd seemed like brothers and sisters. All six of them, she thought with an aching pain. She hadn't thought of the future other than to do everything in her power not to disappoint the don. Spain? What she would give to return to Charleston to the tolerant little family that had taken her in.

The thought startled her. True, there was little in Pensacola, but her memories of Charleston were fading. Nothing waited for her there. Mama had no family, she was told, and she could not burden the McKays again. The large family who had sheltered her had not celebrated her departure but surely it had eased their burden. As much as she missed it all, she belonged to no one there. She knew nothing of Spain.

"There's no need to send me away," she blustered. "Besides, I cannot leave you alone."

"Oh, I will not live forever," admitted Don Marcos, "and this is no place for a young woman to find a husband and raise a family." He patted a straw hat down on his head as the carriage bounced along then waved his hand in the air like a baton as if he heard music playing.

Emma's mind swirled with heat and fear. She did not want to be left alone, yet she did not want to go to Spain. Despite feeling imprisoned in the hacienda at times, a part of her loved it here—the clear green-blue water, the white, sugary sand, and the porpoises and the birds. Best of all were her seashells and the moonlight over the bay that shined like a picture no one could ever paint.

Her throat gnarled when she realized how much she did want to stay. Pensacola was her home now. "What about Roseline?"

"Roseline has her own family in Havana," the don reminded her in a kind but firm voice. "Of course, we have had an influx of officers and new merchants from abroad, but there is no one worthy of your rank, and besides, I've not seen anyone turn your little head."

Emma flushed as she knew her rank was only pretended. "If we are having a party on Saturday maybe new neighbors will come."

He gave a small chuckle in answer. All of these years he had not pushed her, although her opportunities to meet young men her age were rare. She'd admired the occasional officer at the fort, but they all seemed to act as if they were beneath her. She could never find the courage to pursue any of them, but perhaps that was because none of them had moved her enough to want to see her life change again.

"I'm sure in time I will find someone who turns my head."

"As I hope," agreed Don Marcos, "but there is little opportunity to meet gentlemen worthy of your hand in this distant outpost, and we have connections in Spain who would welcome you with wide-open arms."

Emma took a gulp of courage. "But my mother, she was not..."

The don's intimate manner dissipated as quickly as the daily rain shower. He exhaled loudly through his nose. "Rest her soul," he said in a stilted manner. Emma's mama was a subject he never broached, and whatever Roseline knew about it, she kept to herself.

Emma felt her eyes glaze over. She stared off at the distant battery jutting up from the barrier island through the rigging of the ships in the harbor. The carriage rattled to a halt, and she peered up miserably at the imposing brick treasury.

"Spain is a beautiful country," Don Marcos assured her. "You will find all of our people there. Your brother is in Madrid, and we have a home in Cuenca. I know you will love it as I once did and always will."

"Yes, Don Marcos."

Satisfied, he climbed down from the carriage in lurching movements. Emma waited a few moments to compose herself. She knew what he really meant. She'd bored him enough at last and was in the way. Why else would he send her to live with relatives even if they pretended she did not exist?

Fear sent a wall of nausea crashing through her gut, and she put a hand to her heart. It was just like Charleston when the McKays told her she would be sent to the southward fringes of the North American continent. After all she had done for them, keeping house and watching the children, they had tired of her, too.

Emma mustered up the courage to keep her eyes from brimming over even as her heart raced with dread. She knew nothing of Spain. It was a different world, and this time the don and Roseline would not be there. She would not leave this country no matter who ruled it. She could not leave this land.

CHAPTER FOUR

Phillip loitered outside an office in the treasury listening for any mumbles about pirates or Captain Redbird and waiting for his currency to be exchanged. He preferred his coins in pounds rather than pesos, and Pensacola was one of the few outposts that could serve him. In addition, he'd offered Señor Baca's friend a small loan to cover his losses—not that it was of great concern to Phillip, but it would certainly win him a few admiring friends.

The pleasant smell of polish perfumed the stuffy hallways, and he wondered if brick kept the building cooler than the oak and palmetto boards that framed many of the haciendas. He leaned back against the wall and crossed his boots at the ankles. The *Mary Alice*, his proper and legal ship was in port again. It would be uncomfortably hot before long, and he had to make an owner's appearance aboard the *Mary Alice* and meet with Billy Page today.

Captain William Page—Billy—was a trusted business partner who enjoyed commandeering *Mary Alice,* but he was too easy on the crew in port. Phillip prayed those on board in the know would say nothing about a pirate crew hiding out in the bayou. His visit would hopefully remind them of the lives and money at stake.

The floor under his feet vibrated, and Phillip glanced down the hall to see a small party of officials striding toward him. Harried-looking men flanked Don Marcos on either side as they led him upstairs to the more private meeting rooms. Phillip straightened so they could pass and dropped his head in acknowledgment. The herd stumbled to a halt when Don Marcos stopped in front of him. His eyes narrowed. "Señor..."

"Oakley," Phillip reminded him.

"Ah, sí. You were at the bonfire and danced with my daughter."

"I did. I hope you enjoyed the celebration."

The don gave a very slight bow. Phillip noticed his daughter two paces back. Although she paled, her jaw stiffened, and she pulled her shoulders back when their gazes met. He slanted his head at her.

"Good morning, Señorita Montego."

Her dark eyes sparked with something unfathomable before she lowered her stare to the floor. Don Marcos glanced over his shoulder. "Señor Oakley, has my daughter not grown into a beautiful woman?"

Phillip glued on a smile. "I have thought so since we were introduced a year or so ago when we discussed your order from Kingston."

"Ah," he recalled. "A small order, yes? A quality shipment of sugar cane for me and my household."

Phillip added, "And coffee if I recall."

The don beamed. "I must have my coffee. It is true. I hope your ship has had no troubles." He did not mention pirates, but Phillip assumed that was his meaning.

"We have been safe and unmolested," he assured the nobleman. Phillip's gaze moved back to Miss Montego before he could stop himself. The don glanced back at his daughter who waited silently as a nodding rose. "Emma's birthday is this Sábado." She smiled at him as if in obedience.

How dutiful, Phillip thought. She looked ready to nod and curtsy at any encouragement from her papa although she did not look happy to be here. Phillip studied her and saw her petite frame tense.

"We are having a fiesta for her birthday," confided the don. "You must join us, yes?" Clearly, Don Marcos wanted as many guests as possible to attend the birthday party for his daughter. Perhaps he hoped to outdo the lieutenant-governor's party.

"Of course," replied Phillip with a bow. "Anything else I have that day will be rearranged."

He'd already intended to attend with Baca and Hidalgo. Now it was official. He had no intention of leaving Pensacola without a final word of warning to Miss Montego. Although the *Mary Alice* had returned from Louisiana, his work here was not done.

Miss Montego's frown told him she was not happy he'd agreed to come to her party, but he dropped another low bow as the group continued down the hall. He leaned forward slightly after the don passed, but she skirted around Phillip without a sideways glance as he grinned from ear to ear. "And how do you do this fine morning," he crooned after her with a wink.

Miss Montego paused and watched the party of men she was following continue down the hall without her. She stepped back against the wall to put space between herself and Phillip's boots. "I am doing well, Mr. Oakley."

"Then I am mistaken. I thought you looked distressed."

Her glance flitted over him then looked away. "I am just overheated from the sun."

He inclined his head. "Are you certain that's all it is? Perhaps you need an ear." He leaned forward, and she pulled her head back as if afraid of him. "I can keep a secret, can you?"

Miss Montego's eyes widened, and Phillip knew she understood his meaning. "I can keep a confidence just fine, thank you very much." Her words came out stilted.

Was she afraid he'd reveal her secret? Or did she suspect there was more to his? Phillip took a quiet breath, hoping she did not sense his taut nerves. There was something like suspicion swirling in her coffee-brown eyes that made him wonder if she had linked his appearance on the beach with the sudden escape of Captain Redbird.

"Good," he managed to blurt in an abrupt tone. "So can I." He let a sly grin slide up one side of his face. "I hope you are enjoying your seashells."

She jerked again, and her cheeks flushed. Her mouth fell open, clamped shut, and she turned on her heels. "Gracias, Mr. Oakley," she blustered and darted away.

Phillip let out a long breath and relaxed. It seemed she would stay quiet for as long as he was in Pensacola. Whether or not she kept her part of the deal after he sailed away remained to be seen.

After admiring her neck while she marched upstairs, Phillip fetched his money and cantered across the breeze-swept street to the harbor where *Mary Alice* was being refitted with a new topsail. The casual chatter across her deck petered out as he strode up the gangplank. The captain was waiting for him.

Captain Page, or Billy, his oldest friend still breathing, had served with Phillip aboard the *HMS Leopard* against his will as a powder boy, too. He later joined Phillip in the small fishing business that evolved into one of trade, several properties, and eventually, the purchase of *Mary Alice*. Named after his mother, Phillip had passed the reins of the merchantman over to Billy when he decided to sail the *Revenge* with his friend's support. In-between escapades helping himself to smaller British vessels, Phillip sailed aboard the *Mary Alice* as owner and guest, as well as other times when it was necessary to overshadow his illicit activities. With Billy on his one side and Chekilli on the other aboard the *Revenge*, Phillip had felt invincible until he'd run into Miss Montego.

He strode into Billy's quarters after greeting the crew and plunked down in a mahogany chair across from a modest desk. Billy pushed the logbook over. "We're still missing Goody and Keene. I suspect they drifted over to the bayou and the camp."

Phillip frowned. "I do prefer all the crew to stay aboard when you're in the harbor. The *Revenge's* men are cleaning her hull and lying low."

Billy made a face. "They prefer their lean-tos on the beach. I'll speak with them should they turn up."

"As will I if I find them in the bayou." Concerned, Phillip set the box of coins on the table. "Here's the pay for the *Mary Alice*. I have our cut under Queenie's protection."

"We set out for the islands tomorrow. Will you stay for the pelt order since it hasn't arrived?"

"Yes," revealed Phillip, thinking of Emma Montego's birth-day party. "I'm waiting for the delivery, and Chekilli is seeing to that. I'll come board and sail out with you when you next return."

Billy thumbed through his logbook and made a note. "And the *Revenge*?"

"With so much time on my hands, in the meantime, I will put her to good use once the search for her is surrendered."

Billy gave a satisfied nod. He understood if Phillip and the crew were captured they would say nothing of the *Mary Alice* and her crew. And if Billy were ever questioned, he would have no answers either. Both crews served the same purpose aboard their different ships, and sometimes they switched positions. The *Mary Alice* brought in legitimate money divided equally between both crews. The *Revenge* took back what the British squeezed from other nations and shared it amongst all of the men on both ships and with those on the edges of civilization without a country, loyalty, or hope. As long as Captain Redbird remained a mystery, everyone profited.

Phillip tried to look unworried about being discovered as he updated Billy on Miss Montego and their deal. He assured his friend he would keep tabs on the don's daughter until everyone escaped Pensacola's waters, even if he had to haunt her courtyard every night.

IT WAS ALL EMMA COULD do to rise from her bed the next day. The don's declaration to send her away shared so casually on their weekly ride together, had left her too upset to face him at dinner or supper. She could only wear a mask so many hours of the day, and the news that she would be sent to Spain made the pretending to be satisfied unbearable.

If there was no way to stay in Pensacola in her little world, there had to be a way to avoid being shipped to Spain where she was sure her cold and distant half-brother would lock her away in a little room. The only answer was Charleston. Perhaps the McKays would take her back until she could sort out a situation. The problem was how to get there. The don would never agree.

"Will you tell me what is the matter now?" pleaded Rosaline, when Emma finally roused herself and slunk over to the blue shutters that overlooked the courtyard. The oranges had grown bigger and brighter. Thinking of them made her dry mouth water.

Rosaline moved the tea tray Betsy had deposited earlier onto the vanity in hopes that Emma would eat something. "Has the don spoken to you?" Emma inquired in a hoarse voice. She dropped down onto her stool before the looking glass.

Roseline met Emma's bleak stare in the reflection. Her friend was a paid companion, but she was all Emma had in the world. Roseline's soft eyes glimmered then looked away. She picked up a comb and began to pull it through Emma's hair.

"He told me yesterday I may return to Havana to visit with my family, and perhaps live there if I wish... and that you are going home."

Emma's throat shrank, and she pressed it with cold fingers.

Roseline continued to glide the comb through her hair. "You are lucky," she assured her in Spanish, "your hair is not too thick and lays flat." She pulled it up. "See what a fair neck you have."

Emma drew in a shaky breath and wet her dry lips. There had been enough tears last night. She could feel her eyes chapped in the corners. She swallowed down a lump, and it hurt. "Will you come with me though?" she choked out, although she knew the answer.

"Arrangements have already been made," Roseline murmured.

A pool of despair formed in Emma's lungs. Roseline had been her friend for more than five years. She'd taught her how to dress, walk, and sit properly, and even how to behave while having tea time with other ladies, although there was never tea. They called it *merienda*.

"You must not worry, Emma. Your *español* is quite good, and your father's name will open doors for you."

It seemed Roseline had no problem seeing Emma go. She set her jaw so she did not well over with watery tears, but when she caught her friend's eye in the looking glass, she saw Roseline's eyes were wet in the corners. Her neck looked splotched, too.

"I don't want to go," Emma blurted, despite her determination to maintain her poise. A sob threatened to escape, and she cupped her hands over her mouth and bowed her head.

Roseline rubbed the back of her neck. "Don't cry now. Don Marcos is feeling his age and only wants to do what's best for you."

Emma rubbed her cheeks and inhaled deeply. It would be easier to force herself to calm now before her stays were laced tight.

"I'm certain there is a little time to change things now," Roseline continued. She began to pin up Emma's hair at the back of her crown. "However, your father would not dare think of sending you across the sea with this Redbird pirate lurking about West Florida. They say he's a gentleman," she spluttered, "but a gentleman doesn't rob and steal."

For some reason, Emma thought of Mr. Oakley and his piercing blue eyes. His skin was so red and tanned he was almost as dark as the don, but it was a different kind of bronzing that made his eyes glow like the moon. Or perhaps it was his hair—a brownish rust shade that looked much like red starfishes under the water. She chewed her lip. What had he been doing out on the shore the night Redbird had disappeared? She needed to know.

When people whispered about pirates, Emma always thought of Blackbeard. The horrid man had haunted the coast decades ago along South Carolina. Pirates like him blew up ships and harbors and ravaged young, helpless maidens.

"How does that look?" Roseline clapped her hands together in an effort to cheer them both up and distract Emma from what lied ahead. Soon, there would be no white sand meeting the green surf, no overbearing pelicans looking sideways at her, no racing white clouds over the endless blue sea for as far as she could see. Her heart shuddered again, but Emma made herself examine her hair and nod in approval for Roseline's benefit.

"Let's try on your new gown for your birthday just one more time," Roseline suggested. "It's a beautiful gown fit for a Spanish lady."

Lady? thought Emma. She didn't feel like a lady. How the McKays would laugh to see her now. She was just a girl. A helpless young maiden. She glanced sideways at Roseline across the room. *Your papa would not dare think of sending you across the sea with this Redbird pirate lurking about...*

ON SATURDAY AFTERNOON, Emma prepared to dress for her birthday dinner in a new bright blue gown that accentuated her silk petticoats. A firm knock roused her away from the looking glass where her untidy hair streamed past her shoulders. She opened it, knowing Roseline would have slipped inside, and found Don Marcos at the threshold looking formal and official in his black attire.

"May I come in?" he asked in Spanish, and she stepped back, speechless at his venturing into her sanctuary after so many years. He looked around the pristine room crowded with fine English furniture and Spanish chests. Her seashells cluttered every available surface.

Emma took a seat at the end of the bed. He seemed to have no inclination to sit but stood looking around the room as if making marks of approval over its contents. He offered a small smile when their eyes met. "I have a gift for you," he announced, and Emma felt her cheeks warm.

"You've already given me so much," she insisted, eyes darting to her jewelry chest full of earbobs and gemstones.

"You are too modest." As if it was his responsibility, Don Marcos reached inside his coat and pulled out a small box. Emma flushed. She had a room and a companion and all she could eat. The don ordered her bolts and bolts of fabric and lace, not to mention shoes from France and fans from the East India Trading Company.

"Thank you," she murmured in Spanish and accepted the box. What could a widowed man, a stranger who called himself a father, offer to his obligatory burden of a daughter? Especially when he'd already given her so much?

Emma opened the ivory box, and her breath caught in her throat at the sight of a brilliant gold bracelet. She raised her eyes in surprise, and he beamed. "You did not have to do this." It was heavy and wide and shined like an Amazon treasure. "I don't know what to say." Truly, she didn't.

There was a small engraving on the inside of the bracelet and when she turned it, Emma managed to decipher a message written in her new language: *Con todo mi corazón*. Her cheeks flushed deeper. Why would he say such a thing? *With all his heart*?

Emma rose to her feet but stopped herself from embracing him when he stiffened. Don Marcos inhaled sharply and then as if in awkward agony, reached out and patted her on the arm. "I thought it would look lovely on you."

"Gracias, Don Marcos."

He gave a curt nod and stood silent with eyes twitching between her and the looking glass behind her. "Well," he mused, "I hope you have a happy birthday and a lovely evening."

"Thank you for the dinner. It's very generous."

"Our friends are happy to come," he insisted, and she bit down the reply that she had no friends besides Roseline. Sadly, the week had also forced her to accept that her companion was only a friend because it was her duty, too.

"Did you know Captain Gonzalez will attend?" The corners of the don's mouth turned up, and Emma looked away unsure of how to respond. Captain Gonzalez was impressive with his dark uniform and golden striped cuffs, but she did not find him particularly handsome—only powerful in his own mind—much like her father and the governor and those in command of Pensacola who strode about on eternal and essential business.

Emma murmured, "I am happy he could attend." It crossed her mind that a husband might keep her in Pensacola, but Captain Gonzalez did not make her feel anything at all. At least she deserved that much, and so did he.

Don Marcos studied her as if hearing her thoughts. "Captain Gonzalez may soon be called back to Havana. Perhaps even Spain. It would be good to have another friend there."

Emma tried awfully hard for her smile to not look like a grimace. Now was not the time to beg Don Marcos to change his mind. She did not want to go to Spain. She could not. He would think her so ungrateful if he knew.

He ducked his head and excused himself from her bed chambers. In five years, he'd never lowered himself to come into her room. Emma turned to the looking glass and examined a sallow complexion with her hair down and eyes dark and solemn. The bracelet looked out of place on her thin arm wearing nothing but a dressing gown.

Blinking in the mirror, she tried to imagine herself with blue eyes like she knew her mama had, but it was difficult. She was no more a reproduction of her mother than she was of her father. She was her own thing, a broken and lonely shell of an orphan from the Carolina low country, with a shadowy bloodline that seemed like a fairytale without a happy ending. Captain Gonzalez could not be seriously interested in her. Besides, his duty was at sea protecting their little settlement from invaders and pirates.

Pirates. Like Redbird. Emma's mind turned sideways and considered the suspicious Mr. Oakley again. How he'd jeered at her when they'd met in the treasury. He acted as if he knew a secret. Well, she was no fool. She knew one, too. If he wasn't involved in the events in the waters around Pensacola, he surely knew something about it. Why else would he have threatened to reveal her midnight walk down to the shore? She was certain he was up to no good.

A blinding idea lit up her mind. If Phillip Oakley could sneak himself into Pensacola like a thief, why couldn't he sneak her out?

EMMA WALKED CALMLY down the stairs with Roseline behind her, but her stomach sank when the rigid gaze of Captain Gonzalez caught her eye. He stood in the crowd below, clapping with everyone else, but there was something hungry about his gaze that went beyond well-wishes.

He must have had some influence on Don Marcos, for he was seated right beside her at dinner and peppered her with questions whenever the don and others were distracted from their obligations to heap her with praise. After cake and a song, they dined on roasted chicken and turkey with heaping plates of rice, a cold soup, and melons from the gardens. Emma could not help but watch the gold bracelet on her wrist catch in the light with her every movement, and Captain Gonzales noticed it, too.

"What a lovely bangle," he observed, and she thanked him. "What does the engraving say?"

Feeling abashed, Emma murmured the expression in a hushed voice, and the captain's face softened despite the thin eyebrows that made his small eyes look rakish. "You are quite loved, Señorita Montego. Of course, he would want you to have such a special thing on your birthday."

Emma thanked him and went back to her cold melon and strips of smoked fish. Beside her, she felt his glances and pretended not to notice. She answered the lieutenant-governor's wife's question about whether or not she had ventured as far as Louisiana, and when Emma explained in her tentative Spanish that she had not, the woman chided Don Marcos who smiled tightly then reminded them of the dangers of the French and Americans on all sides.

Emma excused herself only a few minutes after dinner. She crept upstairs as the party moved into the courtyard with music and clapping that she suspected would evolve into dancing. Roseline followed her upstairs to hurry her back down. With a sigh, Emma refreshed herself then obeyed and braced herself for more smiles and congratulations.

It took great effort not to plod down the stairs. When she reached the last step, Emma noticed two figures speaking at the door to the drawing room, and her breath caught in her throat. Mr. Oakley had come after all. She froze. He'd seemed delighted to receive an invitation.

Emma studied the cad in the bright silk waistcoat with consternation. He looked like he'd just stepped out of a tailor's shop on one of Charleston's cobbled streets. Even without the broad black hat he often wore, she would know the towering stature and broad shoulders anywhere. She narrowed her gaze. Not to mention, the rust-red locks that glowed with streaks of ruby in the light of a bonfire. Redbird indeed.

Her mind poked her instincts, and her instincts prodded her heart to act for herself. No one else would save her, and what was there to fear? She was no longer a child and should embrace her past and present circumstances. Her future depended upon it. Hadn't she survived thus far? Hadn't she grown? It was time for a new deal. She would not be afraid of Mr. Oakley or his secrets.

Roseline nudged her from behind, and Emma circled around the staircase and made her way to the courtyard. To her relief, she saw Captain Gonzales had found something to distract him. She accepted more well-wishes and showed her bracelet to anyone who asked about it. All the while, her mind churned over her secret deal with Mr. Oakley and what awaited her if she was shipped out of Pensacola and loaded onto a galleon in the port of Havana to cross the ocean. Her heart raced with hope—and a nervous terror—over what she must do.

CHAPTER FIVE

The don's house looked like it was on fire from the distance. Torches flamed from every column and pillar. Music echoed from the courtyard. Curious, Phillip accompanied Señor Baca through the great house. There were two long rooms on either side of the front hall. One had a table fit for a king with over a dozen place settings. It was heaped with fruits and sweetbread and other delectables for wandering guests in search of sustenance. Across the dining hall, a drawing room was crammed with chairs and benches, two settees, and a *chaise longue*. A staircase stood at the end of the hall, and an open door led out to a courtyard filled with revelers.

Phillip and Baca joined Hidalgo in the drawing room to greet their host and his friends, then wandered out to the courtyard to look for Miss Montego. They found her in a raised chair watching the dancing and musicians in the cool evening air. The sky overhead looked swathed in violet and indigo curtains. A woman, her constant and ever-present companion, sat beside Miss Montego tapping a fan in her palm. A few other ladies, mostly older and married, mingled around them in lace shawls and low-fitted gowns laughing in quiet murmurs.

Phillip accepted a drink from a servant but stayed on the fringes of the crowd. There had obviously been a dinner earlier in the evening. Miss Montego was flushed from all of the attention. Captain Gonzalez, to Phillip's surprise, stood near her casting long gazes her way. A dance began, and even as the thought passed through Phillip's mind to invite her to stand up with him, he watched the captain make his bows and Miss Montego nodded. The couple danced a *contradanse* around the courtyard as the sky dimmed and hundreds of candles and lanterns beamed even brighter.

Phillip avoided eye contact with the few single women sheathed in silk and damask and examined the flora instead. He couldn't help but study the second floor of the house and make guesses as to where Miss Montego's room might be. She would want a view of the courtyard, he imagined, with its orange and lemon trees, the palms, and a giant magnolia. He was more than familiar enough with it now and could slink inside without worrying about the layout.

His heart tensed. What was he thinking? To creep into the courtyard for a midnight visit with the daughter of Don Marcos would be suicide. It was best for him to stick to his usual routine and behave. The *Mary Alice* had departed without him again. He needed to pass along word to his Creek contacts and see about the pelts, and he should return to the bayou for another visit with Queenie. There was the pirate camp, too. Eventually, they would grow impatient.

Phillip wandered over to an alcove. A fountain spurt water from a stone face carved into the wall of the courtyard. Protected by overhanging tree branches and vines, he slipped closer to admire it. It made a pleasant trickling sound. Sensing someone behind him, he expected Señor Hidalgo to beg him to find the game room. Phillip turned with a proper expression to cover his boredom. To his surprise, Miss Montego stood just a few steps away with a hesitant look on her face. The music grew louder, and she threw a glance over her shoulder then moved closer.

"You are kind to come to my celebration, Mr. Oakley," she acknowledged. There was no trace of an accent, no Spanish lilt to her tone. The stiff pretense of custom and propriety were set aside, and her stare felt steady.

Suspicious, he bowed. "Señorita Montego."

She took a step closer with no expression on her fair features. "Thank you. I'm surprised you are here," she confessed and watched him carefully with dark eyes. "I overheard someone tell my father the *Mary Alice* has left Pensacola.

He felt his gaze sharpen. "I am staying longer," he explained. Did she suspect he was Captain Redbird? That the *Mary Alice* was his pirate ship in disguise? Ha! He was no fool. He wouldn't take that sort of risk. "I trust you do not mind?"

"I do not. In fact, I'm happy you've come."

"You are?"

She stared like she wanted to say more. Something about it was suggestive, and he wondered at her sudden change of heart. He reached for her arm, and she didn't resist or look frightened. Phillip guided her among the potted plants, his mind simmering with distrust over her supposed pleasure in seeing him. "I understand you are from the colonies," he pried although it was generally known.

"I am. Charleston."

"Ah, then, see, we were once neighbors. I grew up in Savannah."

She looked at him in surprise, and he thought he saw a flash of camaraderie in her gaze. "Tell me about your home," he dared.

After a pause, Miss Montego's arm relaxed slightly in his, and she told Phillip about a family that raised her in their small house on the edge of town. Listing the McKay children one by one, she shared how she helped care for them when she was not cleaning or cooking with their mother or following their papa into the low country to explore or watch him fish. It was a frank story for a woman of such wealth and respect.

Listening carefully, Phillip thought the wistful tale made it sound like she wished to return. Her presence in Pensacola all made sense when she shared the story of Roseline's arrival on a ship that carried her away from all she'd ever known. She trailed off after giggling about her first few attempts at Spanish.

"You speak it quite well now," he assured her.

"I thank you," she murmured as if she had forgotten herself. She seemed much less frightened of him now and almost trusting. Perhaps she had forgiven him for surprising and threatening her under the light of the moon. It seemed as good a time as any for him to make his move and give her a final reminder. He looked around for any eavesdroppers and pulled her into the shadows of the alcove. "About our deal," Phillip began in a grave whisper.

"Yes, about that," she interrupted.

The woman with the olive skin and matching gown swished into the alcove. Sensing her companion about to join them, Miss Montego stepped forward into his arms and said under her breath, "Meet me at the palm grove before dawn," then turned on her heel and fell into the embrace of her lady friend.

The companion looked over Miss Montego's shoulder at Phillip warily, but Miss Montego took her by the arm and led her into the throng that now clapped and sang as they parted like the Red Sea for the pair to walk between them. He stared after the ladies in astonishment and saw Captain Gonzalez watching from the crowd as if he'd noticed their intimate conversation. Phillip lowered his eyes and drifted back to the fountain and its strange carving of the sun. A ripple of fascination skipped down his spine.

The beautiful Emma Montego, who rarely spoke to anyone unless spoken to, who watched everyone with her dark, unreadable eyes and did not smile further than the corners of her lips, had become quite the chatterbox before inviting him to visit her in her courtyard again under the light of the moon. How clandestine. And very unladylike.

The idea of it almost made him breathless, and he wondered if she'd felt the same surge of attraction that he'd felt when they faced one another down under the tree along the shore. No. Surely, this was false hope. She probably had questions about what he was up to. Would she mention the pirate Redbird?

Phillip's chest squeezed. If she had figured it out, why speak to him and not go to Don Marcos? He remembered her urgent whisper and smiled to himself. Perhaps she was more American than Spanish, after all. He thought of Queenie and her unabashed sensibilities that required him to pay a toll for crossing through her bayou. Perhaps young and clever Miss Montego wanted a cut of the pirates' take in exchange for her silence, too.

Or, maybe, perhaps, he had it all wrong and she had decided she liked him.

Phillip reached up and plucked a purple-pink blossom from a bougainvillea vine and twirled it between his thumb and finger. He grinned despite the headache and nightmares her interference was causing him because he couldn't help admiring her.

EMMA LINGERED DOWNSTAIRS until the last guest departed, whispered goodnight and thank you to Don Marcos, and trudged to her chambers thinking desperately of a way to stay awake through the night. Dawn could not be that far away, she surmised, as a yawning Roseline helped her undress after fetching another cup of cold coffee without questions.

Emma waited until Roseline retired then rested in a chair by the window watching the courtyard sink into peaceful darkness. Tendrils of smoke from the extinguished fires in the kitchen house drifted across the yard like lost spirits. She took a deep breath and exhaled, stiffening only when she heard Roseline turn in her bed in the room next door.

Her good and loyal companion had stayed at her side for as much as she'd deemed appropriate throughout the party. It puzzled Emma how Roseline could share her thoughts and opinions so freely when they were alone but how conservative she became, almost like a shadow, when the lieutenant-governor and other wives of the settlement came around. She behaved as if she did not deserve to be in their company because she was unmarried and not widowed.

Emma had not been a witness to the upper echelons of society in Charleston, but she had a general idea of how things worked; at least she thought she had until the don whisked her around the continent and across a sea to this strange sandy paradise. She knew should she step foot away from Pensacola, she would no longer be the don's daughter and treated like a princess, she would be Miss Emma Montego again, a single woman of no fortune with a mysterious benefactor who kept a roof over her head and shared his foreign name. A nobody. Emma rather missed being nobody.

She wrapped her silk robe around herself for modesty's sake and reclined in the uncomfortable chair at her desk afraid to go to bed. After the night deepened, and the hours stretched to their final limits, she stood at last and stretched. Outside the window, she examined the sky and empty courtyard then tiptoed down the stairs and out the back door.

There was no one in the kitchen house. No one upstairs looking out. The don's study windows were inky black. She tiptoed across the yard stopping only to peer into the alcove at the severe face on the fountain trickling out of the wall that had mesmerized Mr. Oakley. Or if she was correct, Captain Redbird.

Emma trod lightly over the hard-packed sand between the bricks in the courtyard to the gate. Glancing toward the orange trees and remembering with a flood of tingling feelings, Mr. Oakley's embrace beneath a tree and the moon, she squared her shoulders. He was not a gentleman after all that, and if he was truly what she suspected, she could be in danger. But... he was an American and a stranger like her in this place. He had to understand why she could not be sent away to a foreign continent that could never be her home.

Hearing no one, Emma slipped out onto the footpath and walked toward the distant beach in darkness with ears sharp and nerves on edge. After several long and tense minutes, she stopped at the palm grove between her and the shore. The ebb and flow of the water crooned like a lullaby as it shushed and sighed on and off the sand. Her toe nudged something hard, and she picked up a piece of shell. It looked broken. Sometimes those were her favorite.

"Are you looking for me?"

Emma nearly jumped out of her skin. Behind her from the shadows, Mr. Oakley stepped out like an apparition. The moon was bright and nearly full so she could see him better than before. He'd shed the coat he'd worn to the party, but silk threads glistened in his waistcoat under the moonlight. He put a hand on his hip.

"I've lost an entire night's sleep," he complained in a droll tone, "dutifully waiting for the Señorita Montego to come out for her nightly swim."

"I'm not swimming," Emma said in a low tone.

"We're not?"

She felt her cheeks go hot at the very idea. "What? No."

"I'm disappointed."

Emma resisted the urge to cross her arms and glare. He was teasing her like they were friends. She surveyed the gentle and inviting surf spreading shells across the wet sand but stepped back into the darkness of the footpath.

Mr. Oakley held out his hand like he had a gift. "Here. Take it."

Emma raised a brow but offered her palm. He dropped a shell into it. She couldn't see the colors or patterns, but it felt scalloped and heavy.

"I – thank you." She studied it both pleased and confused.

"Are we going to walk?"

"What? I don't know, I - I needed to meet you," she explained.

"I'm happy to do so. We did not get to dance." Mr. Oakley's voice sounded soft.

Flustered, Emma blurted, "I needed to meet because I want to make a new deal."

Even though she could hardly see him in the shadows, Emma saw him startle. He choked out, "A new deal? We had an agreement. I tell no one you wander around Pensacola at night in your dressing gown, and you tell no one you met me on the footpath."

Emma took a breath and gambled. "Yes." Her heart began to thump with anxiety, and she clenched her hands. "You did not come to Pensacola aboard the *Mary Alice* that day," she guessed, cursing the tremors in her voice. "I asked Betsy about it. She saw the *Mary Alice* come in. She was at the market. She does not remember that you got off. She said Captain Page was aboard."

"That's because he's the captain. I'm the owner, and I sail at my convenience."

Emma swallowed and took another breath. "If you were aboard, you would have disembarked right away, but my Betsy did not see you. I could have asked Don Marcos, but I supposed he would not know."

Mr. Oakley snatched her wrist and stepped out into the moonlight. "And did you?" His voice sounded like a soft growl.

Emma tugged away, relieved that he allowed it. "No. I had second thoughts. I thought perhaps I might be right. The don was up late with the lieutenant-governor that night. He comes to him for advice. There was an attack on one of our ships by pirates. They disappeared beyond Santa Rosa. And then I met you."

She tried to read his face in the darkness. Only half of it was revealed by a beam of the blue moon. He stared into her eyes like he wanted to push her back up against a tree and strangle her this time around.

Emma shivered, sensing the danger she'd created for herself. One moment Mr. Oakley was charming her with smiles, and the next, threatening her with cold glares. Was she a fool to try to do this on her own? She thought of the other option, of being herded onto a ship and trapped for months at sea without Roseline. A strange land. An unwelcoming family. "I have no choice," she winced. "I must know."

Mr. Oakley leaned closer until their noses touched. "Tell me you did not tell your papa. Say you kept our deal."

"I did," she gulped. This close to his warm, broad chest and bright eyes reflecting the moon made her feel breathless. "I kept our deal, but I need your help."

Mr. Oakley exhaled. She saw his hunched shoulders relax. "My help?"

Emma took a deep breath and braced herself. "You are the pirate Redbird. I know it. I saw you sneak into town. I saw your sword and your wide hat with the feather in it. I can only guess it was red, as red as your hair."

Mr. Oakley reared back like she'd slapped him. His piercing gaze never left hers, but his breathing stilled. She could almost feel his mind racing. Was he angry? Afraid? It had to be true. His reaction was the final proof of what she already knew.

"Pray tell, Miss Montego, what do you want for your silence?" His deep voice sounded hollow and carried an undercurrent of something treacherous beneath its confession.

Emma held back a gasp of surprise. She was right after all, and this could be a mistake. Her heart had told her one thing, but she should have listened to her mind. Mr. Oakley, or Captain Redbird as it were, could easily cut her down under the cover of night. His giant heavy hands could wrap around her throat and squeeze the life out of her.

Was he a murderer? The Pirate Redbird was called a gentleman pirate, who said "please" and "thank you" and humiliated his victims by making them undress and cast their clothing overboard after he robbed them blind. Yet he still carried a sword. She had seen it. Emma glanced down at her silk robe. Would he shame her the same way after he took her life for threatening to reveal him?

"What do you want?" he repeated in a stabbing tone.

A gust rolled in from off the sea and swirled the robe around Emma's legs. It teased the loose strands of hair at her temples that had escaped their braid. Heart pounding, she took a deep breath and whispered, "I want you to kidnap me."

PHILLIP STARED AT THE woman in front of him until he realized his mouth hung open. Before he could ask her to repeat herself, Miss Montego added in a hushed burst, "Don

Marcos is sending me to Spain. I have a brother there. He's older and has a family, but—" She stopped and took a panicked gulp of air. "We have never met, and I can tell from his letters he has no room for me in his life."

Stunned, Phillip studied her in the moonlight. It shined across her face making her look like a silvery ghost with Spanish eyes. Her cheekbones sat remarkably high. If he leaned closer, he suspected he would be able to see her long lashes even in the darkness.

"You want me to kidnap you?" he prodded. If she did not keep talking he might kiss her. He might kiss her anyway. He was already done for. She knew who he was, and she was trying to blackmail him into some dreadful bargain. If he was going to hang as a pirate, he might as well enjoy his final few moments as a free man.

He watched her head wag with sadness in the darkness. "I need to get to Charleston. It's as close to a home as I've ever had, and if I can't stay here..." Her bosom heaved up and down with anxiety.

"Do you want to stay?" Phillip asked. Why would she not? It was a beautiful land—hot—but it was only unbearable for a few months out of the year. If it weren't for the grasping hands of the British and his own countrymen, it would be paradise. "Do you?"

Miss Montego — Emma—stopped her panicked breaths. "Why yes, I like it here very much," she replied in a whisper, "but I am not completely Spanish, and my father is an old man. He has done so much for me, I cannot trouble him any longer. I'm a burden."

She made a choking noise that sounded like a stifled cry then tore her gaze away to stare at the moon. "I was a burden on the family who took me in as an infant." He watched her gaze drop to the silvery sparkling ocean. "I would stay if there were a way."

Phillip stepped back to put space between him and this bewitching lady-child. "Tell your father you don't wish to go."

Her voice broke. "He wants me to meet his other children and to – to marry well."

Phillip snorted. He knew she would be lucky to find a match in Charleston even with the don's fortune—if he didn't cut her off. The same would happen in Madrid. "You think you will marry well in Spain with your American blood?"

Her little mouth made a small *o*. "It doesn't matter," she whispered in a fierce tone. "I won't go to Spain. I'll go to Charleston and work out something else."

Phillip laughed quietly. "So this is your ingenious solution? Blackmail me into taking you?"

"You are Redbird, aren't you?"

He surveyed the beach around them, wondering if witnesses or guards were hiding in the gangling pines. "I am, but you are Emma Montego, beloved daughter of Don Marcos."

She sniffed at his description of her. "I am not beloved," she mourned, "I'm an ornament, a token of something he must pay back for whatever life he led in the colonies."

"Your mother?"

Miss Montego widened the gap between them. "Do we have a deal or not?"

Phillip threw his head back and gave a short, barking laugh, and she shushed him. "How do you propose I kidnap you?" He looked back toward the rooflines of the settlement. "I am in Pensacola waiting for a delivery of pelts to load onto the *Mary Alice* when she returns, and then I go."

He watched the girl take a steady nervous breath. "That's not your ship?"

"I told you it was."

"I mean your pirate ship."

He chuckled. "If I told you I had a pirate ship, I'd have to do more than kidnap you, *Señorita* Montego."

"Don't call me that," she countered, "and I know you have one. You must." She took a step toward the footpath to leave him, but her figure wavered like her knees might go out from under her. She was afraid, he realized, terrified of him and what she was asking him to do.

"Go home, Miss Montego," said Phillip in a lazy tone. "Talk earnestly with Don Marcos. Tell him you wish to stay and that you will find someone here to marry when the time comes." He grinned at her. "I understand Captain Gonzalez comes from an upstanding family and a long line of officers straight back to the Armada."

She swept a defiant chin over her shoulder. "I will not marry a Spaniard," she retorted. "It did nothing for my mama, and now I must fend for myself!" The young woman fled back up the path, kicking sand up with her heels like an angry little mustang. Phillip bolted after her, his heart thudding with a concern that erased his amusement. "But you will keep my secret? We still have a deal?"

Miss Montego spun around and surprised him with her vehemence. Perhaps the American girl did not recognize she'd inherited her father's reputed temper. She was quite brave—and clever. "No, the deal is off."

Phillip swept her up in his arms and strode into the prickly underbrush out of earshot of any trespassers. She grabbed his shoulders and kicked her legs until he let her down. Before she could escape, he snatched her elbows and pulled her against him close enough to feel her heart galloping through the thin muslin and silk of her nightclothes.

"Our original bargain still stands, *Señorita*," he said in a voice thick with warning.

Miss Montego trembled in his hands. "You must help me before they send me away," she insisted.

She was determined. He'd give her that much. With a sudden jerk that made her gasp, Phillip lifted her so they were nose to nose, and her slippers didn't reach the ground. Gazing into her eyes so closely was like a pleasant midnight dream. Somewhere inside him, Phillip felt the darkest recess of a forgotten path suddenly flame, and his heart dropped into his stomach.

He set her gently down onto the ground. "I'll think about it," he surrendered in a begrudging tone. It was the best he could do to disguise the swirl of emotions she stirred in him. Had he not once felt just as lost? His olive branch seemed to pacify her for the moment.

"Do you promise?" She gazed up at him unruffled by how close they stood together.

"I promise." Phillip kept his tone gruff and inched away from her. When she released a sigh of relief, he held up a hand to halt any assumptions. "I said I will consider it, although how I'll whisk you out from under the nose of your father and the Spanish Navy, I've no idea. And by the by, I have no way to get you as far as Charleston. The Indies, or perhaps Havana, will have to do and then there would be other arrangements. You'll be on your own."

She studied him with rounded eyes that reminded him of a pleading kitten. "I can trust you then."

Phillip realized he was giving in. "From one American to another, I will do my very best." He smirked and offered his hand, and she looked at him in surprise then gingerly took it. As soon as he felt her slender fingers against his skin, he turned her hand over and kissed the top of it. When he looked up with a smirk, her surprise had turned to shock. "But of course with this new deal, Miss Montego," he warned, "I get something, too."

CHAPTER SIX

As soon as Phillip Oakley released her, Emma dashed up the path using dappled moonlight as her guide. The skin on the top of her hand burned like the midday sun radiating off the sand. Breezes from the gulf ruffled through leaves and fronds, cooling the glow that coursed through her veins. How could she feel so hot and cool at the same time? she wondered, but she knew. That man. That *pirate*. He made her feel capable and brave and... grown up. He seemed to understand her. It was perplexing and frustrating. He was a criminal!

Emma slowed as she approached the don's courtyard. She was more than likely safe now. She'd found a way to avoid going to Spain, and Phillip Oakley had not harmed a hair on her head, although he'd frightened her for a moment. It was a charade, she knew now, just like the play-acting he did in town pretending to be a merchant conducting business here.

He'd agreed with some reluctance, or at least he said he would think about it. She pushed open the gate, wincing at the groan it made over the insects' song and the distant surf. It was essential to Mr. Oakley's safety and perhaps others, Emma imagined, that she keep his secret. She latched the gate shut behind her with a satisfied exhale. He had no choice but to help her. Someway. Somehow.

Feeling hopeful and a wee bit smug, Emma strode across the courtyard to duck back into the house. The sky was no longer black-blue, but indigo, a sign that a gleaming band of sunshine would soon rise over the eastern horizon. She froze with one sand-filled shoe in the air at the outline of someone at the door of the kitchen house. Betsy stood on the single step, with her skirts pulled up in one hand and the other raising a small lantern to see who was in the yard. Her eyes looked wide like she'd been startled. The lamp wavered in her hand, and Emma felt her questions.

She swallowed, heart racing, and made herself continue across the courtyard with slow, unhurried steps. A prickle of perspiration broke out across her back. "Betsy," Emma remarked as if surprised, "Good morning."

"*Buenos dias.*" The woman released her fistful of apron, but her forehead crinkled with confusion. Emma realized she'd spoken in English. She'd forgotten who she was completely, but it mattered little because Betsy spoke several tongues. Her examination of Emma shifted back to the orange trees and garden gate. "Are you hungry this early?"

"No. I mean, yes. Wait. I'm just thirsty." Emma gave a soft chuckle and looked innocently over her shoulder. "Yes, I was up, and I thought I would have some water from the fountain, and then I heard something—"

Betsy's eyes rounded.

"A bird," blurted Emma. "I thought I heard a red, no, a – a chicken!"

Betsy stared at Emma like she was babbling in tongues she didn't understand.

"So," finished Emma, "I just stepped out." She forced a light laugh. "I didn't mean to startle you, and my—" she peered toward the eastern sky, "why are you not still abed? We were up all night, weren't we?" She took a deep breath and blew it out, realizing she was trembling from lack of sleep, fright over Betsy, and perhaps, Mr. Oakley planting a kiss on her hand.

"Do you want coffee?" The question hung heavy in the air with doubt.

Fatigue suddenly found its way onto Emma's shoulders and sank into them. "Oh, Betsy, no. I'm still tired." A yawn crept up her throat, and Emma let it out. "See how tired." She shook her head like it was a shame. "I'm going back to bed. No coffee, but thank you."

She tried to sound cheerful as she escaped to the house to avoid any more questions. What more could she say? Her hair was mussed around her face, her wrap hardly straight, and her slippers oozed with sand. She did not turn around to see if Betsy was still watching. Emma was sure guilt was written all over her face.

A FOG TOOK OVER HIS mind once Emma Montego raced out of sight. Phillip walked to the beach within view of the fort and took a swim as dawn broke. Redressing in the bushes, he strode into town nodding at the early risers in the settlement—a servant, shopkeepers, and even a few customers at the market. He hurried past them on foot, his skin drying quickly in the summer air.

Two women carrying baskets heaped with eggs stopped to stare a little too curiously, and he instinctively pulled down his hat, but it wasn't there. He hadn't worn one into the underbrush. After a surge of panic, Phillip recalled the red in his hair was hardly noticeable when it was wet, and he was not wearing the cocked hat with dyed turkey feathers he donned aboard the *Revenge*. He offered a genteel nod and continued on his way to the widow's cottage where he slipped inside as if in no hurry.

Phillip let out a groan and leaned back against the latched door. His eyes burned with salt and fatigue, but his mind raced with anxiety. What had she been thinking, the wretch? To draw him out so near to dawn and at the same spot he had caught her before?

He collapsed onto his narrow bed in his damp clothes and shut his eyes. Kidnap her? Sail into the deepest and most protected harbor on the West Florida coast and drag her from the hacienda of Don Marcos? No problem. Only he was Mr. Phillip Oakley, the merchant, *and* Redbird the pirate. The *Revenge* would be seen by all of Pensacola, not to mention, Captain Gonzalez. He'd never sail out of the gulf in one piece.

Phillip flipped over onto his side unable to stay awake any longer. Nothing ever happened that hadn't happened before, Queenie often said. There was a solution to every problem because it'd already been sorted out. It was as good as Shakespeare. Phillip needed to see her, but how to be discreet?

His heavy mind stumbled around for answers. He was in town to receive animal skins. Perhaps a visit with the friendly native people in the area was in order—as far as anyone else needed to know. He could mention it in passing to Hidalgo before he left town and then skirt across the territory to the bayou.

Queenie would know what to do.

Phillip's tired mind melted into a sleep with pictures of sea and sun and then into the cool darkness of a breezy Pensacola night. To his delight, as he drifted away, Emma Montego was there waiting for him.

"UP!" SHARP PINE NEEDLES stabbed him in the face.

"Ow!" Phillip winced and drew back in alarm then collapsed with a groan. "Queenie," he moaned. He tried to roll over in the drooping hammock, but there was nowhere to go. She rapped him across the head again with her broom.

"Get up, Phillip-boy." Queenie sounded more irritated than yesterday when he'd come whistling through the bayou on foot with a musket and haversack slung over his shoulder. She thumped him on the rump with her foot. "Get your hammock out of my kitchen," she grumped, and he sat up woozily and looked around.

"I slung it where there was room." Phillip scrambled out of the bedding and stood up to stretch his back. He'd hung the hammock in the low corner of Queenie's cabin alongside the table she stocked with an assortment of projects during the day. Queenie smacked down a platter of seasoned and blackened prickly pear onto the table.

"I see you've been out of the bayou," he remarked, reaching for it, but she slapped his hand.

"We pray first," she reminded him, and he bowed his head while trying to hold back a smile.

After long-winded and praiseworthy chants of gratitude, she passed him a small bowl, and he served himself with his fingers. The long strips of cactus were charred as he liked them, but she surprised him by offering extra-long strips of dried meat that made his mouth water as soon as it hit his tongue.

"Where'd you get beef?" he wondered with a furrowed brow and full mouth.

She raised her brows. "Chekilli," she replied with a shrug. They both knew there were few buccans in the bayou, and the only cattle he knew of belonged to the lieutenant-governor and Don Marcos north of the settlement.

Phillip closed his eyes and savored the satisfying taste of Spanish beef with a *hmmph* noise. Queenie clucked her tongue. "Chekilli did not say you would come back here."

"I thought I would drop by on my way to the camp." Phillip stared at his cactus and hoped she would brew the coffee beans he'd brought to please her.

"You miss Queenie Oba," she observed through a muffled mouthful of breakfast, "but no, Phillip-boy. You can't fly away and come back and fly away and come back without a word or a warning." She slapped the table with a flat hand. "If you don't stop this sneaking about, you're going to sleep for good with Davy Jones. Why don't you stay in the bayou?"

"Now Queenie," complained Phillip, "you know Kingston is my home. Sort of." He wrinkled his brow at his British address. "I could not stay when England turned the settlement over in '81. I'm lucky they've let the *Mary Alice* go in and out since then, but at least with the new treaty to resolve border disputes I'm officially welcome now."

Queenie sniffed. "A treaty for white men. What about Queenie and Chekilli?"

"It was just for the governments," he stammered.

"The Treaty of Friendship, Limits, and Navigation Between Spain and the United States," Queenie recited. She frowned knowingly. "Long words hide deep intentions."

"I think it's respectable enough. At least it will keep the Redcoats out of Florida for now and the Mississippi, too."

She shrugged at Phillip's excuse. "Treaties don't mean anything to a man that wants land. They'll always want more." She glowered. "Ask Chekilli."

"I know," Phillip admitted. "Heavens, I've seen it." He looked around the small cabin and appreciated its safety and security in the hot, Florida bog. *Where will they go, I wonder?* he asked himself. The Creeks had been pushed out of Pensacola and now from most of West Florida. They were trapped by the Americans on three sides with Spain lying between them and the sea. Their sea. He sighed. When he thought about it too much, it hurt his head.

"Did you come to see me to talk politics?" Queenie wondered. Her serious question was ruined by a quick upturn of her mouth into her cheek. "Or bargains?"

"Bargains?"

"You made a deal." Her lips stretched into a suggestive toothy grin. "What was it?"

Did she know about Miss Montego? How? "I see Chekilli brought you more than beef," he complained.

She guffawed. "I know when a woman is stirring the pot. It smells like life but tastes like death."

Phillip glanced at the collection of dried animal parts hanging around her neck. "And what do the bones tell you? Am I still going to disappear into the night?"

Queenie's amusement disappeared as the curves in her cheeks melted away. "Pensacola is nothing but trouble for you now. Why not stay in the bayou with me and your pirates?"

"I have the *Mary Alice* to deal with."

"Give it to your trusted friend," Queenie suggested, "the boy, Billy Page. You can't be a trader and a pirate at the same time. One is toil and trouble. The other is sure death."

The smoked beef soured on Phillip's tongue. "If I were to lose the *Revenge*, I'd have no way to escape if I was discovered, and they would hang me."

"So? You despise the Redcoats. Stay in Florida."

"With the Spanish? Here? And if there was war?"

Queenie stroked her necklace. "War never ends. It just rests awhile. Your Americans will be in Pensacola someday." She looked around and grimaced at her prediction.

"You'd be safe here, Queenie," Phillip assured her, "in the bayou."

She snorted, and he understood her doubts that Americans would ever see her as a free woman even if the Spanish had. He pushed his bowl away. She could never leave the bayou. She would never trust her freedom to another man or country again.

"I could give up the *Mary Alice*," he supposed, "if it came to that, but I rather like having the safety net. Who knew a farm boy would have a head for business?"

"Thanks to my teaching you."

Phillip reached out and covered her hand on the table. "I see no point in collecting more boats and bigger houses to fill with things that mean nothing to me. It's family, after all, that makes a home." This he'd learned when the British had destroyed his. "They took my treasures, now I take theirs, and all the while living on their very island in Kingston." He laughed.

"Stop your pirating," warned Queenie. "Get a letter of Marque."

"From the British? Never. Spain maybe. And what am I to the Americans? It's been years, I'm nobody there."

Queenie pointed at him with a bony knuckle. "You're somebody here." She clasped his hand and put it to her heart. "You're somebody to me."

Warmth and gratitude washed over Phillip so strongly it almost made his eyes water. He matched her gaze and let the peaceful energy flow between them. She tilted her head. "You've been thinking about more than your mamma and papa. You want a family now, too."

He pulled his hand away with a forced chuckle. "Me? I'm pirating. The British made me what I am, Queenie." He shoved away a picture of Emma Montego—a fine prospect—from his mind. "They made me fire cannons on my countrymen then dumped me here on this flat frontier."

"You were a fine fisherman," she raised a brow at him, "and a fool to leave Queenie to be a big man in Kingston."

"What choice did I have not to go with them to Jamaica? There was more work," Phillip excused himself, "more opportunity. They don't know an American from a Londoner if you talk right. I understand you not wanting to go with me—"

Queenie pulled back. "Back to that place?" she grunted. "Where it's heaven for one man it's hell for a hundred more."

He slumped his shoulders. "I'm sorry. I understand."

"You don't. You couldn't." She sat back with a weighted sigh. "What matters to me now, Phillip-boy, is that you stop prancing around this Spanish harbor like you're some kind of gentleman and get out until the pirate is forgotten. There's nothing but trouble with that *guardacosta* coming to stay, and the Spanish man's daughter has noticed you."

"Her name is Emma." Phillip looked down at his fingers. "She's an American like me. Well, half. She's the don's daughter."

"I know who she is," declared Queenie in a confident tone. "She's divided like you are and doesn't know who she is any more than you, so get out now before you find yourself in leg irons."

Phillip hesitated then took a deep breath. "That's why I've come, Queenie. She's too observant and smart for her own good. She knows."

"She knows what?" Queenie's eyes widened impossibly larger. "Was that the deal? She knows your Redbird?"

He grimaced and shook his head *yes*.

Queenie rolled her gaze to the ceiling and slapped her chest as if her heart had betrayed her. "What are you going to do now, Phillip? I told you a storm was coming!"

He bit his lip. Explaining he was being blackmailed by a young woman who wanted to escape a voyage to Spain was too embarrassing. "I have no choice, daughter of a don or not, so—" he took a deep breath, "I'm going to kidnap her and smuggle her back to America."

A DAY LATER, EMMA CLIMBED out of bed and walked to the window. She assumed no one would mention today was a day of celebration in the new United States. It was only twenty years old, a big achievement, unlike Emma who was three years older and trapped. At least she would be if Mr. Oakley didn't come through.

She gazed down into the courtyard she thought of as hers. If she wasn't in the drawing room with Roseline, riding with Don Marcos in the carriage, or napping or writing in her chambers, she was in the courtyard admiring the palms and the blueness of the sky with its thick heavenly clouds. And then, of course, there were the fruit trees.

There was so much about Pensacola Emma was beginning to realize she dearly loved more than giant, colorful seashells. Despite sometimes feeling like a prisoner than a guest of Don Marcos, she was blessed to have more than a leaky roof over her head and her own room, not to mention her own bed, for she had slept with two little girls in the McKays' home.

Unlike some of the difficult times in the low country, food was plentiful here. Roseline had taught Emma Spanish and helped her improve her figures, and now she embroidered for pleasure rather than sewing out of necessity. She had free time unlike when she washed, dressed, fed, and schooled the little ones with the McKay's worn Bible.

The sky looked clear which meant another hot day. Emma could not help but examine the courtyard gate. It was shut. She squinted and studied the smooth ground. No seashells were waiting near it. Perhaps that meant Mr. Oakley—or Captain Redbird—had not changed his mind. She hoped. She hadn't honestly believed she had any chance of convincing him to abduct her in the night, but she'd guessed right on two counts: he did not harm her although he'd been incredulous, and he'd agreed to it in the end. Hadn't he?

The kiss? Why had he done such a thing? Her cheeks heated at the thought of it just as they had burned all day yesterday. She could not put it from her mind. He was so tall and so handsome with his ruddy skin, bronze locks, and penetrating eyes. They were as blue as the distant sea where it grew deep and dangerous...

The shell he'd slipped into her hand sat on the vanity. The very corner of it was chipped, she noticed. Had he? Did he have a tender spot in his heart for broken things, too? She shook herself and banished the silly thoughts. She never thought Emma Montego would be one to act like such a simpleton. Who would have known she'd fawn over a man? Especially after caring for so many little McKay boys with their dirty cheeks, loud shouts, and propensity for trouble.

No one had paid her any mind in Charleston although there were plenty of gentlemen who rode about in fine carriages through the cobblestoned streets. None but the tailor's son seemed to notice her, but he did nothing to make her swoon in the way the other girls whispered about. Of course, things had changed when Don Marcos sent for her. Her brothers and sisters *oohed* and *awed* like she was a lost princess. Neighbors had stared with admiration. He'd sent money and other fine things for her with Roseline and for her adopted family, too.

Emma stood on her toes and gazed over the trees and rooftops to study the distant water. It looked as blue and clear as a diamond, nothing like the cold brown waters of Charleston's harbor. But it was the same ocean that ebbed and flowed onto the Carolina shores, and soon it would carry her back to the only home she'd ever known like a small, lost seashell.

Once upon a time, she'd thought all of this a dream, and now she knew it was. She would not spend the rest of her life imprisoned in a brother's house in Spain until some wealthy old nobleman lowered himself to marry a woman of mixed blood. If she could not stay in Pensacola, she would return to the city of her birth and make a living of some sort. Surely, the McKays would help.

Emma sighed and turned to begin her morning routines. The gold bracelet shimmered from its box, and she floated across the room and sat down to stare at herself in the looking glass. Picking up the don's expensive and personal gift, she realized its value and knew it would be of good use once she was on her own.

With all my heart. She studied the engraving, and guilt pricked her conscience. It was the most personal gift he'd ever given her, and she wondered why he was sending her away if he felt any affection for her at all.

Footsteps came up the stairs, and Emma recognized Betsy's cadence that she knew by heart. It moved across the hall and stopped in front of the door. The servant knocked lightly, and out of a habit that would never die no matter how rich the don made her, Emma stood and went to open it.

Betsy looked at her in surprise. "Good morning. I have your coffee and melons," she announced.

Emma smiled and thanked her. It was hard to meet her eyes. She'd avoided Betsy all yesterday because of the guilt that might show on her face, but today she felt better rested. "I can take it," Emma insisted, not wanting the servant to slip inside of her room. Things had been moved and stacked in different corners as she considered what must stay and what must go when the ominous pirate Redbird crept in and stole her away. She wondered if perhaps she should just meet him in the garden.

Another rap sounded on the door, and Emma jumped. Roseline peered around it and smiled upon seeing her awake. "Betsy said you were up early today."

"I could hardly sleep." It was true. Every time Emma heard a noise in the night, she'd tensed and listened with burning ears. She fully expected Redbird to appear with a motley crew of ne'er-do-wells at any moment. They'd be carrying a suffocating sack to stuff her into before they crept back to their pirate ship.

"Well, if you are not too tired, let us have our breakfast in the courtyard. I should finish telling you about Señora Perez and my visit yesterday while you were sleeping."

Emma carried her tray to the bed then plopped down hoping Roseline would sit beside her as she sometimes did. "I can't wait," she mused, "tell me now."

Pleased, Roseline padded across the room and eased herself onto the ticked mattress. "I took the don's gift to Señorita Perez. She is still puffy and pale and all that, but my!" She held up two fingers. "Two babies, she had, and at the same time!" Roseline announced this as if it were a magnificent feat. "They are so tiny, so precious." She reclined back onto the bed with a covetous sigh. "What good fortune to have two little ones."

It didn't sound fortuitous, but Emma was happy their neighbor had survived both a pregnancy and a delivery in such a wild place. "Two babies? She's fortunate they are both here on time and in good health."

Roseline smiled in agreement. "As you will find yourself to-day, my friend. Fortunate, I mean."

"Why is that?" A sudden stab of guilt pierced Emma's soul. This woman was her friend, her one confidant, and treated her like she was family. Emma hadn't been loved so much by any-one else in so many years and yet she would have to betray her. Poor Roseline. Emma resisted the urge to lean over and embrace her.

"Come now? Why do you look so stricken?"

"Oh, no," Emma shook her head, "it's only you say I am lucky today, but I am lucky every day." She winced at her weak excuse.

"Well, you should know I overheard the don speaking with the lieutenant-governor about your journey to Spain. It has been decided that Captain Gonzalez shall take you as far as Havana, and I shall, too."

Roseline's eyes brightened. "See? This is good news for you and me. You will know someone as far as Havana."

"Can you not go with me to Spain?" Emma pleaded again. She fought the urge to tell Roseline about Mr. Oakley and Captain Redbird and the deal. How could Don Marcos not see that this was all a horrible mistake?

"No, dear heart. You know I cannot." Roseline set her lips in a sad, grim line. "Please don't fret. You will have a maid to help you and keep you company along the way. See? We will write letters, and you can tell me about all of your adventures in the homeland."

"But Roseline," whispered Emma, trying not to cry, "what will you do when I go away?"

"Hush now," urged Roseline. "I have family there and will find work as I always do."

"As another companion?"

"Yes," thought Roseline with a searching look. She sounded pleased. "Perhaps, or I may return here. I can sew and mend."

A thick clump of jealousy settled in Emma's stomach.

"Now," clapped Roseline, jumping up and taking Emma's empty plate from her hands, "you know you must not eat in your bed, Emma dear. Why has Betsy not kept up? Your shoes are all out, and why are your shells everywhere?" Roseline did a slow turn around the room eyeing the collection Emma had sorted and spread across the window sill and vanity. She would only allow herself to take five back to Charleston, but choosing even one from among them seemed impossible.

"I just set them out to admire them," explained Emma, feeling horrible again. How Roseline would worry when she believed Emma had been kidnapped by villainous pirates and taken away. Would she grieve for her? Would the don?

"You silly girl," said Roseline with a handsome smile, "there will always be seashells. You can take all of them with you to Spain."

Emma tried to look mollified, and it seemed to work. Roseline arranged her pretty face with a more serious expression. "This morning, Don Marcos wishes to speak to you in his study as he does at the start of every week, and should he mention your passage on the *León* to Havana with Captain Gonzalez, do act surprised."

Emma nodded obediently although it wrenched her heart. She had little time before her departure, she suspected. She wanted to shout and stomp her feet. She did not want to go but no one would listen. Her ludicrous idea to have a pirate kidnap her could be a mistake. What if he stranded her on a deserted cay?

Her breath hitched in her chest, and Emma put a hand to her throat. Even if she survived this mad plot, Roseline would be horrified to think her dead. And what if Mr. Oakley was caught? He'd be tortured and hung. Emma would still be sent to Spain although now she would be ruined. She sank back down onto the bed feeling weak in the knees. Perhaps Don Marcos would consider sending her to a convent instead. She gulped.

"Come along now, dear Emma," called Roseline from across the hall. "We must not keep the don waiting."

DON MARCOS HUDDLED over his desk with a ledger in front of him and a large monocle in one eye. As Emma crept into the study, she realized this was her last chance to convince him she should not go to Spain. She had to succeed, or she would have to carry through the deal with the wily, red-headed buccaneer in their midst.

With his head bowed, Emma thought the don's hair looked more white than silver, and thinner, too. He coughed deep in his chest then sat back. His eyes widened in surprise upon noticing her, but he collected himself when she approached the chair across from his desk.

"*Buenos dias,* Don Marcos."

He removed his seeing glass and offered a nod of approval. "Have you recovered from your birthday? I'm sorry it exhausted you so."

"Oh, no," she appeased him, "I am well now. I know I slept a great deal of yesterday, but I feel much better."

"I'm glad. Your health was of concern at Mass, but I told everyone you were simply resting." He closed the ledger and opened a small diary. From across the desk, Emma could see large and scrawling handwriting that showed his eyesight was failing.

"Roseline said you wished to speak with me."

It was the same weekly routine they'd carried on for several years, and something familiar he seemed to enjoy. Today it felt different. Emma's hands were damp and trembled slightly.

"Yes, as it is Monday I wanted to go over our appointments. I intend to go out to the grazing land this week with Pablo to check on the cattle."

With a thrumming heart, Emma raised her brows to act interested. Perhaps if he knew how much she was willing to learn, he'd change his mind about sending her off. "Would you like me to accompany you?"

"It's too hot," he replied. "I don't wish you to become over-heated and fall ill."

As careful as she handled eggshells, Emma said, "I am young and in good health, Don Marcos. I worry the heat is too much for you."

"I must go," he insisted, "we are missing a number of cattle. Apologies mean nothing, and I am greatly concerned. This is the second time in three months a few of the herd have disappeared."

Emma squeezed her clasped hands. Her heart thudded like heavy footsteps. "I have only to call on Señora Perez with Roseline," she informed him in a halting voice. "Will you go to the treasury today?"

"I had not planned to trouble you," he mused, "but I will take you along if you wish to go. Perhaps we can go down to the waterfront. The lieutenant-governor's wife has taken ill, and I do not wish you to be around anyone with something catching so we must not call."

"I am happy to help if they need me," Emma offered, "always I am. I hope you will allow me to assist you as well when you need it."

His mouth stretched into its weak smile. "You would be willing to help an old man? You are a good daughter indeed."

Emma caught her breath. Now was the time. "I do worry about leaving you, Don Marcos, and going so far away while you no one to watch over you."

"Oh," he chided her, "I have taken care of myself for many years, and there are Betsy and Pablo."

"A servant and a secretary are advantageous to be sure, but they are not true family." Emma held her breath. He seemed touched that she thought of him as family now, but it was hard to tell for sure through his impassive facade.

"That is why I must send you to Spain," he said at last, "so you will have someone that is your own blood to depend upon and to trust."

Emma almost fell back in frustration. She flung her hands to each side of the chair and gripped it until it hurt. "Don Marcos, the truth of the matter is, the only family I've ever known is in Charleston except for you here in Pensacola. I don't want to go away," she confessed, her throat straining to keep her emotions under control. He stared like he was shocked, and she swallowed before taking another breath to continue.

"I cannot bear the thought of going. I want to stay with you. The settlement is growing and there is a treaty with the United States now. Surely I will have the opportunity to wed someone to whom you approve in time, but for now, our hacienda here in Pensacola is all that I need."

Breathless and out of words and afraid if she continued she'd break down and beg, Emma stopped and waited. She squeezed the chair again, her anxious heart making her chest rise and fall like she'd come running from the other room.

Don Marcos straightened. He steepled his fingers and rested his elbows on the edge of his desk. He looked like a king pondering from his throne. With a soft intake of breath, his dark eyes found hers. "I am old, Emma, and will not live forever."

Avoiding her surprised and sympathetic gaze, the don glanced down at his book, and once more, Emma realized she was nothing more than a possession to him.

"You, however, have your entire life before you, and I must see you are safe and provided for. You are my responsibility, and Spain is our home."

His words felt like blows to her stomach. Emma felt her shoulders droop, and she nearly slumped out of the chair. Her hopes sank. He would go to the very edges of the frontier to check on his cattle and make sure they were safe. He would send her to Spain and put another tic mark in his ledger. She realized she was shrinking and tried to speak. Was there any use?

"Run along now, Emma," he instructed her. "I asked Betsy to serve us *meriendo* in the courtyard this afternoon. I want to show you how the orchard is coming along so you will know how well we did here in West Florida when you see the glorious orchards in Spain.

For a moment, Emma couldn't move. There was no escape. She was nothing more than an heirloom to be shipped off like cargo. The father she had always dreamed of having would never be, and her hope that the don would come to love and see her for whom she was was ruined. She gave a sharp nod and scraped the chair back as she hurried from the room.

CHAPTER SEVEN

Phillip paddled out of the bayou in the shifty pirogue and circled the bay until he reached a finger of land east of Santa Rosa island. The crew hid out here in a tree-shrouded forest of oaks and pines with prickly grasses. Hiding his small craft in a long bed of sea ferns, he picked up a narrow game trail and made his way inland until he spotted a red scarf tied in the top of a tree. He paused and shuffled his feet in the pebbly sand.

Before long, the shrill imitation of a bird echoed through the woods, and he knew he'd been spotted. He ducked his head and fingered his machete as he squeezed past low branches until it opened up into a camp. Two dozen men, minus a soul or two, milled about cleaning fish from the morning catch. A few others dozed up against tree trunks shaded from the merciless sun. There was little breeze in the hideaway, but they had little choice as good caves were hard to come by unless one traveled further inland.

Chekilli crouched under a canvas awning slung between two trees, and whatever he was boiling did not smell good. The men around him came to their feet and saluted. Some greeted Phillip kindly and with relief.

He could tell they were ready to get under sail. At least at sea, there was a breeze and the possibility of good fortune. In this place near the bayou, besides caring for their vessel and making repairs, there was little to do except hunt, drink, and sleep. Everyone kept a wide berth from Pensacola. Everyone except him and Chekilli when it was necessary.

"Mr. Ortega, sir," teased Phillip when he reached the stink brewing under Chekilli's awning. His first mate gave him a slight bow then dropped back to his work. The shade was not much cooler than the sun. "I wonder that you weren't out swimming," admitted Phillip. He sat down across from him and peered in the pot.

"The rain's coming," the Creek murmured.

Phillip looked up at the clear blue sky. "It rains every day."

"Lightening," mumbled Chekilli.

Phillip did not ask how his friend knew the danger would accompany today's shower. He leaned back on his palms. "Queenie requests that you bring her some type of fish," he murmured. "They are too small in the bayou."

Chekilli looked up and smiled with a straight row of teeth that was missing one. "She just wants another key deer."

Phillip looked around. "I see hides but nothing fresh. Is there plenty enough?"

"Fish, crabs, oysters, and some persimmons."

"I should have brought oranges, I'm sorry," apologized Phillip. He thought of the don's fruit trees in his courtyard.

Chekilli shrugged it off. He was not as picky as his captain. Most of the men were content with lime, ship's biscuit, and whatever could be drawn from the sea. Phillip peered through the tendril of smoke snaking above the pot. "What are you boiling?' he asked with a curled lip.

"Dye." Chekilli stirred it again. "I boil the leaves and root until the red comes out. Then we soak our shirts and handkerchiefs."

"Ah," Phillip understood. "For the Redbird crew."

Chekilli nodded. "They have to pay me in pounds or pesos. I don't need fish or rabbits, I can catch my own food."

"Aren't you industrious?" Phillip glanced at the others. The men were so used to him coming and going they'd relaxed and gone back to their business. He ran a tight ship only when necessary. At least his time aboard Britannica's man-o-wars had taught him something. He took a soft breath and said, "I have news about Miss Montego."

Chekilli's head snapped up so fast his dark hair rippled down his back. "She keeps the deal?" His voice echoed with concern.

"Yes. I had a word with her before I left under the pretense of checking on my order of pelts."

"Then we will say nothing about her midnight walks," said Chekilli with an amused grin and toss of his head. "I do not understand how a woman can be shamed for taking a walk along the shore without a companion."

"I was her companion," snorted Phillip back. "I almost scared the life out of her. The privileged have their ideas, you know."

"Nobleman," growled Chekilli in disgust. "A woman should be able to hunt and fish before she's even considered marriageable."

"Miss Montego was raised in the colonies. I bet she can do a great deal more than hunt seashells, but as the don's daughter she cannot even leave her courtyard."

Chekilli wrinkled his forehead. "She's clever we must allow, for she has us cornered like mice." He sat back, and Phillip saw unease on his face. He couldn't bear to admit she'd wrangled out his secret identity. They were in more danger than anyone knew.

Phillip cleared his throat. "She is being sent away to Spain. The don is concerned for her safety and virtue here in Pensacola." The man mumbled something under his breath Phillip didn't try to interpret. Instead, he told Chekilli, "She has asked me to kidnap her."

Chekilli threw his head back and released a howl of laughter. He slapped his hands on his thighs through his breeches. "That would be fitting and easy."

"I'm glad you feel that way."

Chekilli dropped the stained stirring stick into the grainy dirt and crossed his arms over his chest. "You are going to kidnap a Spanish girl?"

"She's a woman," Phillip insisted, admitting to himself there were years between them, "and only half a Spaniard so she does not want to go to Spain."

"What will you do with her?"

"You mean what will *we* do with her."

Chekilli's dark almond-shaped eyes widened with interest. "You want me to help you kidnap a woman?"

"You're already a pirate."

Chekilli laughed. "A buccaneer, but yes, I'm happy to take back what little I can recover from the Redcoats."

"I spoke with Queenie," continued Phillip. "She suggests that we do not take her from Pensacola after all. They might search the bayou, and people might be... discovered."

"The wise one," Chekilli agreed. "Yes, she's right, and for our friends in the north fiercely gripping their lands, there might be trouble."

"I didn't even think of that," admitted Phillip. "I'm sorry. You're right. Anyway, I think the best thing to do is let them ship her out on whatever merchantman they decide."

"And?"

Phillip smiled. "We have a ship, too. The *Revenge* can intercept her."

"What about the *guardacosta*?"

Phillip tried to keep his face impassive. He knew little about Captain Gonzalez. "All that I have been able to gather about the captain is that he comes from a family of some standing with great wealth and has insatiable ambitions."

"He is young."

"Young and foolish. Just because one can bark orders and knows his knots doesn't mean he can sail the Florida coast. He's fresh and inexperienced here. By the time he receives word and searches for us, we'll be long gone."

"Mmm." This seemed to soothe Chekilli's concerns somewhat. He picked up his stirring stick. "What will we do with the señorita once we kidnap her?"

"Take her to Kingston. I'll need to make arrangements once we reach the islands. She'll be taken to the States. That's where she wants to go."

Chekilli frowned at the obstacle. Phillip lifted his shoulders in a helpless shrug. "If we can get her to Kingston we can find another merchantman and have her smuggled aboard. It will be a long voyage, but she's determined not to go to Spain even if she must leave Pensacola."

"She has people in America?" Chekilli sounded empathetic.

"Not anymore from what I understand."

"What will she do?"

"I don't know."

Chekilli exhaled in annoyance at his unanswered questions. Truth be told, Phillip had not thought that far ahead. Maybe he should have. What prospects could a half-Spanish woman find in Charleston with no family and no inheritance or support from a don?

"I have no choice but to help her," Phillip grumbled in frustration. "If we don't do something, we might be revealed. It's kidnap the don's daughter or make sail and run never to return."

"But she saw you," Chekilli frowned. "She knows your name and who you are."

"I could live with that," Phillip insisted. "Kingston would not be missed. Let them try to hunt us down in the Caribbean. I know the Leewards as well as this place, but it's Billy I worry for—and the crew of the *Mary Alice*. One word, one small confession, and everyone would hang and all on account of me."

"And because of this girl."

"Yes." Phillip sighed. "That is why we must plan our route tonight and have the men ready at a moment's notice. As soon as Miss Montego leaves Pensacola, we are going to chase her ship down, board it, and drag her onto the *Revenge*."

EMMA FRETTED IN THE drawing room with Roseline for days following the don's pronouncement and her hopeless submission. Her nerves felt taut with the rays of sunrise each morning after waiting and wondering all night if Redbird would show. She worried about what he would ask in return and prayed there would be no guns. No violence. She slept with the door slightly ajar and that was if she slept at all.

Phillip Oakley had disappeared. At least she had not seen him about, and when she asked Betsy if she'd seen the owner of the *Mary Alice* while at the market, the servant shook her head. In one moment, Emma was sure he would surprise her; in the next, she was furious and certain he had fled Pensacola with no intention of honoring their deal.

"How is this?" Roseline held up an admirable ruffle on the petticoat she was finishing for her ward.

"Um? Oh, it's lovely."

It was a black, silk *basquina* that she promised everyone would admire when Emma wore it to church. With her black veils and rosary, it made Emma feel like she was attending a funeral when she dressed for their Sunday services, but this, too, was a part of her new life she was trying to understand if not for the don's sake, then for the McKays' who had been devout Catholics.

She returned to hemming a gown she was expected to wear at sea—an indigo-dyed cut of linen that would keep her cool and comfortable and endure spots and stains. A rumble of activity on the sandy street outside came to a stop in front of the hacienda, and Emma's needle hesitated in the air.

Roseline leaned forward in her swishing linen and peered through the louvers of the shutter. She settled back in her seat. "It looks like the don has a guest," she murmured, reminding Emma that she should call for Betsy to prepare some sort of refreshment.

Emma set down her sewing and picked up a fan to stir the air. What she would give to throw on her old bergère she'd treasured in Charleston, grab a parasol, and traipse down to the grove of trees at the shoreline for shade and a breeze.

Betsy pulled her from her wistful thoughts with a light rap on the door frame. She curtsied and presented Captain Gonzalez. Emma looked up in surprise. He walked into the room with his usual, self-assured gait and stopped a few paces away. She rose to her feet, glancing at Roseline who said, "The don is in his study, Captain Gonzalez. Would you like me to announce you?" She glanced sideways at Emma, who wondered where on earth Betsy had disappeared to.

"No, thank you," he murmured in Spanish. His hat was missing, probably handed to the housekeeper. Today he wore no wig, and Emma surmised that it was too hot, but she thought he looked better without it. She studied his long aquiline nose. His brown eyes met hers with a penetrating look.

Emma felt herself drop down to a curtsy. For a moment, she was an orphaned young woman again.

"Good day, Señorita Montego. It's lovely with generous clouds in the heavens, and the sea is calm." He cleared his throat and turned to Roseline. "I have asked the don if I might stroll with Señorita Montego to the waterfront, and he has given his permission."

Emma's heart lurched in surprise. Had Don Marcos not said he wished her to go to Spain because there was no one for her here? She felt her cheeks flush at the attention. Roseline nudged her with an elbow.

"Thank you, Captain," Emma breathed, lowering her gaze to the floor. It fell from her lips before she thought it through, but she felt her companion's approval and sensed the officer's relief. It was not like she could mean anything to him, although she knew he was taking her to Havana soon. Surely he would not pursue her. She felt nothing for him, not in that way.

He gave a slight bow, refused any refreshment, and with a tense smile, Emma went upstairs to gather a wide-brimmed hat and parasol. After informing the don of her intention, which he approved of with a permissive nod, she hurried downstairs to escape the confines of the house she so rarely escaped. Agreeing to walk with Captain Gonzalez made her feel slightly guilty. A stroll within view of the water and any breeze was always welcome. She hoped the captain did not think any more of it.

They ambled down the narrow lane south toward the harbor. Occasionally, a neighbor or officer from the guard greeted them. Emma grimaced as curious stares roved over her. Ignoring them, the captain conversed about the summer heat and daily rain showers that never lasted. He motioned toward empty yardarms in the harbor. "We have rolled our canvas tight should the winds pick up again."

Emma squinted. "Do you think it will storm later? Don Marcos says he can smell when it will be a terrible blow."

"Gauging from the breakers and lack of porpoises this morning, I suspect a good blow is on its way," the captain mused. He turned his head to examine her. "Though I could be wrong. The weather is unpredictable here, and I do not mean to distress you. It won't be too terrible, I think."

Emma suppressed a smile. "Captain Gonzalez, I lived in Charleston half my life. The weather here is a little different to be sure, but I'm not afraid of a storm. I've weathered enough of them."

He seemed to grasp her meaning and slipped an arm through hers so they walked closer together. His familiarity startled her, but Emma decided to see it as an act of friendship and that he wished to feel more comfortable.

"Your Spanish comes along very well," he complimented her. "You seem to like living on the coast here in New Spain."

"My feelings have changed of late to be sure," Emma admitted. "It was quite foreign in the beginning, but I have come to realize I love sand as white as snow, and I don't mind the flat expanse because I can see forever. I do like to see what's coming." *Like pirates*, she inwardly winced.

Captain Gonzalez gave a muffled chuckle. "It is much different from Madrid and my home there; even different than Havana I must say, but it's an island, of course." He wiped at his brow from beneath his cocked hat. "I do think perhaps it's hotter though."

"You are lucky to live on the water," Emma approved. They came to the harbor wall, and she gazed across the water at the battery. "There is little breeze in the don's house."

"Have you ever traveled out of the settlement?"

"Only a few times," she admitted. "Don Marcos worries continually about war parties from inland and invaders along the coast."

"Like the pirates," suggested the captain.

His thoughtful words made Emma's heart stumble. She cleared her throat to disguise the sharp breath they made her take. "I have no fear of pirates," she managed to say. It was true. She was not afraid of the pirate Redbird. Phillip Oakley had never harmed her, and the stories she'd heard were not too terrible. She knew in her heart he wasn't a murderer but...

As if reading her mind, Captain Gonzalez shared, "Redbird sails up and down this coast when he's not irritating every merchantman north of the Indies." He examined her like the information might frighten her. "You need not worry though, the Navy is gathering reports and evidence, and it won't be long before we track him down."

Emma looked away to disguise her alarm. "I understand he is called a gentleman," she managed to say.

Captain Gonzalez sniffed. "What gentleman peppers another man's ship with grapeshot then relieves him of his possessions at gunpoint?"

"Oh, I see what you mean." Emma glanced away to avoid his questioning gaze. Mr. Oakley had warned her he'd want something in exchange for more than her silence about his pirating. Perhaps a few details of the *guardacosta* would do. She tried to pay closer attention.

A large shout from the fort drew their attention. "Come see," said the captain, "they are doing their exercises."

Arm in arm, she followed Captain Gonzalez along the harbor wall listening as he pointed out the *León* and explained her tonnage and number of cannon and crew. The breeze picked up in earnest, and scuttling clouds overhead grew thicker and began to move faster.

When they reached the fort, Emma saw soldiers lined up to practice their swordsmanship. Each wielded a wide sword, or *espada ancha*. With no warning, the front of her petticoat flipped up in a gust, and she hurried to press it down with an embarrassed chuckle.

"I should hold onto my hat with both hands at this point," the captain said, putting her at ease. "I don't want to have to swim for it."

Emma looked at the waves rocking back and forth in the harbor. "Would you?" she teased.

"I have jumped overboard many times to save the silliest things." He leaned closer and admitted, "Once my cat."

She laughed in surprise. "I find that unusual yet heroic. I hope any cat you take to sea in the future will know how to swim."

He smiled as if proud he'd impressed her at last. "I no longer have that devoted fellow, but I have the *León* now." They looked back at the gunship bobbing on the water.

"And she is quite the cat," agreed Emma. He beamed, and she tried to smile, but the *León* concerned her. How fast did it sail? Could it catch the *Revenge*? Was the *Mary Alice* the *Revenge* in disguise? It was a smaller ship and did not carry as near as many cannons as the *León*. And where was Mr. Oakley?

The clash of iron pulled her attention back to the fort. Games were afoot, and the captain looked sorry he was not participating with his crew. "I should let you get back to your business, Captain Gonzalez," suggested Emma. To accentuate her words, a low rumble of thunder boomed across the sky.

"Of course." He tore his gaze away from the fencing. "I did not mean to keep you so long in the sun nor did I intend to have you walk home in the rain."

She gave him a brief nod, and he pivoted back toward the market place with her on his arm to escort her back up Charlotte Street. "I am happy you walked with me today," Captain

Gonzalez confided. "I needed to clear my head what with all the business afoot."

She gave him a curious glance.

"Havana," he explained. Emma's heart sank. He seemed as intent as the don to carry her away. "I know how difficult it is to travel alone," he maintained.

"Yes," murmured Emma. It was obvious he wanted to soothe her reluctance to broach the subject.

"I thought we might get to know one another before we depart."

She gave a small peek to meet his eyes in some semblance of being polite.

"It is less than a fortnight away," he reminded her.

"And so soon." Emma tried to disguise her distress. Less than a month! The don had been evasive about the exact date of her departure. Within weeks, her life would flip pages, and once again, she was not the one turning them. Would Redbird and his pirate band ever come? She squeezed her parasol

"Did you know," wondered the officer with a light laugh, "my family has a cottage in Cuenca. It will be no strange thing if we should see each other once I finish my duty and return home."

What did he mean by it? Struggling for something to say, Emma could only murmur, "What a comfort."

"I would very much like to see you again after Havana I am sure."

"Oh, Captain," jested Emma, "I'm sure after having me aboard your *guardacosta* you will be finished with women aboard your ships."

"It's unusual, yes, and unexpected," he concurred, jarring her by agreeing so readily, "but there are no shipboard superstitions in Cuenca," he reminded her. "Only castles and churches and fine countryside. It will be a pleasure to take up an acquaintance again." She felt him glance sideways at her but kept her gaze straight ahead.

The hacienda seemed leagues away. Emma tried to pick up her pace without looking like she wanted to run back to the drawing room. To her relief and horror, a stranger flew around the corner of a shop almost plowing her over. The captain stepped back in offense with a hand that reached for the hilt of his sword, and Emma stumbled backward over her skirts.

"Captain Gonzalez!" exclaimed the intruder, "I do apologize. And Señorita! Forgive me."

Mr. Oakley picked up the parcel he'd dropped and gave them both an apologetic bow. "Pardon me for rushing about without looking where I'm going." He met Emma's stare for only the briefest moment, his vivid charade of innocence not fooling her at all.

Well, look who's returned, she wanted to trumpet, but she clamped her lips tight. Captain Redbird had returned to Pensacola and was up to something yet again—and it appeared to have nothing to do with helping her escape.

THE CRASH INTO THE strolling captain and his lady was a plan that formed in Phillip's mind the moment he left the tavern. He'd received a message the pelts had arrived at the small trading post northeast of the settlement and set off to the treasury estimating what taxes his exports would cost him. It was difficult to hand over the money since he had a way around paying tariffs, but they had to do everything possible to keep up appearances for Billy and the *Mary Alice's* sake.

Afterward, Phillip wandered over to a clapboard tavern frequented by sailors and soldiers to eavesdrop, but then he'd spied Miss Montego and the *guardacosta* captain in a leisurely stroll down the street as if they were sweethearts. A pang of envy came as sharp as a needle of panic and both pierced his chest. What was she sharing with the Spanish captain? Could she be trusted? And why did he feel so possessive over a woman who was practically blackmailing him?

Phillip gave a deep bow to Captain Gonzales. "Forgive me," he apologized to them both. "I was in a hurry to return home before the storm hit," he hinted with a glance at Miss Montego. "I did not watch where I was going."

"Mr. Oakley," mumbled Miss Montego with a shallow curtsy. Their gazes met, and Phillip did not miss the look of irritation in her eyes. She looked disappointed. Angry.

"Señorita Montego," he drawled, "I see you have recovered from your birthday celebrations. How concerned your father seemed when you became so fatigued afterward."

"I recovered soon enough," she assured him in a tight voice.

"Did you? I'm happy to hear it. It must have felt like you stayed up all the night through."

Fear sparked in her eyes, and he couldn't resist giving her a wicked grin before turning to Captain Gonzalez. "We have not been formally introduced," he admitted in a polite tone.

The captain glanced at Miss Montego. "Oh yes," she blurted, remembering her manners. She hesitated as if unsure of superiority then turned to the naval captain smiling more than necessary. "Captain Gonzalez, may I present Mr. Oakley of Kingston? He is a trader and owner of the *Mary Alice* who enters the harbor on occasion."

Phillip didn't blink but bowed, although he considered himself above a Spanish *guardacosta* captain. But of course, not everyone was aware of his financial holdings in Jamaica, not even little Miss Emma. In his opinion, money trumped ancestry in the new world every time.

"Señor Oakley," acknowledged Captain Gonzalez. "I believe I saw your ship a few weeks ago."

"Yes," agreed Phillip. "She was in and out, but I have stayed to wait on pelts promised from traders north of the settlement. They are late."

"Ah, I see," mused Captain Gonzalez in broken English. Phillip's explanation seemed to settle a question in his mind. "You have a home in Jamaica?" he assumed.

"I do and here as well. I find it more convenient and habitable than renting a place in the New Orleans outpost."

"Your ship returns for you when business there is done?" The captain furrowed his brow.

"That is right. I do not command her," Phillip explained, should the man take note of his reddish hair. "Though I do see the logbooks and work amicably with her officers when I'm aboard."

There was another grumble of thunder. Captain Gonzalez frowned. "And your captain? Is he an American?"

"Captain Page might be considered an American," admitted Phillip, his mind scrambling, "but he served on a British ship in the war." He waited while the Spaniard pondered this revelation. Any American with a ship in these waters would be under suspicion by a naval commander with Captain Redbird about.

"I see," Captain Gonzalez said at last. He reached for Miss Montego's arm again as if she belonged to him. "Well, I hope your business here in Pensacola is successful." There was no sincerity in his tone. "I should return Señorita Montego to her father."

"*Sí.*" Phillip glanced at the somber clouds overhead. "If it does not rain, it will soon be too hot for even shells to rest upon the shore." He sent Miss Montego a pointed look. They needed to talk. A midnight meeting was in order.

She swept her gaze away. The captain looked confused. He gave a short, stiff smile as Phillip bowed again then stepped back for them to pass.

"Oh, Mr. Oakley," called Captain Gonzalez, stopping abruptly. "Has your good ship had any problems with pirates on the coast?"

Phillip froze but shook it off with a sharp breath as his mind raced ahead of his words. "Why, no, none at all." He met the captain's gaze with a sincere stare, resisting the urge to blink.

"Indeed? How very curious. Curious, indeed."

"And why is that?" Phillip caught himself shifting his stance before he could stop himself.

The polite smile on Captain Gonzalez's face stiffened. "Many a merchantman has been accosted by this mysterious pirate, Redbird. Surely you have heard of him?"

A few tentative drops of rain splattered down as Phillip struggled to keep his face impassive. "In the ports here and there, but little else. We have not seen anything of the like aboard the *Mary Alice*."

"Hmm." Captain Gonzalez started to turn away but changed his mind again. "Perhaps it is because you are an American."

Phillip shrugged and let his irritation show through as water began to sprinkle from the sky. "Who would know? We fly British colors. I don't believe a pirate has regard for anyone other than his own."

"That is true," agreed Captain Gonzalez. He gave Phillip a calculated examination before wheeling about on his boot heel. "Goodbye then." He patted Miss Montego's hand. "Come along, Señorita," he coaxed, "before you get wet and catch a cold."

They hurried off between the raindrops as spiny fingers squeezed at his heart. Phillip crossed the street and took another path to the gardens and his little abode—as far away from the hacienda of Don Marcos as he could get.

CHAPTER EIGHT

Emma escaped to her room as soon as Captain Gonzalez released her in the drawing room. She changed for the evening meal and kept her head down as the heavens thundered and Don Marcos ate silently while his secretary jabbered on. She wished Pablo did not dine with them so often, but perhaps it was best since it had been decided she would go away. There was little left to say to anyone anymore.

Giving the gentlemen their time alone at the table, Emma departed with a polite curtsy along with Roseline to the drawing room. She stared into a flickering candle. Mr. Oakley had reappeared even when his ship had not. Where did he go, she wondered?

With a petulant frown, she crossed the room to the window that overlooked the street. She'd peeked down into the courtyard while dressing for dinner. There were no seashells waiting as there'd been before. She wondered why Mr. Oakley bothered to hint at it. Surely he wanted to meet with her. Perhaps he would explain why she had not been carried away by pirates before now.

"Emma?"

Roseline sat by the dark fireplace with her hands clasped together. "Are you troubled? Ill?"

Emma shook her head.

"I only ask because you were so quiet at supper. Did you enjoy your walk to the shore with Captain Gonzalez? I thought that you might ask him to dine with us."

Emma dropped her chin in regret. "To be honest, Roseline, I did not think of it." She gave her a guilty stare. "There is so much on my mind with us leaving soon."

"Yes. Come and sit with me." Wrapping her lace shawl around her, Roseline set her hand under her chin and gave Emma a silly smile.

"What?"

"It has been some time since a gentleman has called on you," she teased.

"Oh," Emma remarked with a dry laugh, "there is nothing to it, I assure you."

Roseline looked disappointed. "And why not? He is kind and gentlemanly, not to mention, wealthy and connected."

Emma felt like a horrible snob, but she lifted her shoulder in a careless shrug. "He is a second son or why else would he be in the Navy?"

"But he is wealthy," argued Roseline, "and will receive some sort of inheritance along with his prize money."

"Prize money?"

"Yes, the pay he receives when he captures an enemy ship. I'm sure the captain does not have a great deal of time to entertain women with his post, so you must be flattered he bestowed some of it upon you."

She was not flattered, Emma admitted to herself. Did that make her prideful and vain? "What difference does it make?" she mumbled then looked over at Roseline with a spark of hope. "Do you think it would change the don's mind if I had a suitor?"

Roseline looked away with a downturned mouth. "I suppose not. He is determined to send you to the homeland, and to be honest," she admitted, "if Captain Gonzalez were to declare any intentions, he would send you to Spain once you were wed."

"Wed?" The word curdled on Emma's tongue. "I have no intention of marrying a *guardacosta's* captain," she declared then hunched her shoulders. "I guess it's shameful of me to accept his invitations to dance and go on walks, but I thought he was only being friendly."

"I imagine there is more to it than that," warned Roseline in a low tone, "for captains are busy men."

"He said he wanted to get to know me better since I will be aboard his ship as far as Havana."

Roseline looked at Emma pointedly. "I'm sure he is looking forward to the trip."

"I have no intention of settling on Captain Gonzalez, and he won't change my mind on the way," Emma promised.

Roseline laughed softly. "If you say so, but I have to confess after so many years I hoped to see you fall in love before we part."

"Oh, Roseline." Emma felt tired. Her mind diverted to Mr. Oakley, and to her consternation, it made her palms tingle. He'd run smack into her on the street, and the steadying hand he'd placed on her arm to stop her from tripping had felt like falling—from a tree, a ship's mast, maybe even a star. It'd only lasted seconds, but just a touch or the briefest glance from the man filled her head and heart with the most foreign of longings.

"Love," hissed Emma bitterly. "I wouldn't know it, Roseline." She shrugged so tightly it pinched her shoulders. "I had no mama, no true brothers or sisters—no family—and the McKays were happy to ship me off after all," she muttered. "Don Marcos does not love me, of course, but I am—"

"Oh, now," interrupted Roseline. "Your papa loves you very much, Emma."

Emma sucked in a breath of surprise. "The don?" she wondered. "He hardly knows me, even after nearly six years." She looked down at her silk gown fit for a ball in Charleston, and here she wore it for light evening fare at home.

"Perhaps it is not that you do not have love," Roseline suggested, "but that you don't understand or recognize it."

Emma's heart creaked with a small and bitter pain. She knew love, but only from general observations. She glanced toward the window and saw the storm shower had dispersed. Why had Mr. Oakley not fulfilled his part of the deal? Time was running short. She turned to Roseline and worked up a yawn. "Forgive me, Roseline," she begged in a low tone, "but I am fatigued and must go on to bed. She knew she would not sleep at all. The shelly shore was calling and so was a pirate.

PHILLIP PACED HIS ROOM beside a rope-framed bed that sank low in the middle and kept him from sleeping well. He and Chekilli had their plan, but Billy would need to be informed of it. Another problem was passing the information along to Miss Montego. She had not blinked when he mentioned the shells, and he suspected she thought he was teasing her rather than hinting to meet him at their spot along the shoreline.

Should he go? She seemed upset with him, and he could only guess at it. He huffed in frustration and flopped down onto the corner of the bed. The woman had altered their bargain and he had left town abruptly. He'd spread the rumor he was off to check on his pelts. She could not know he had fled to the bayou to talk things over with Queenie and the men at the camp. Kidnapping a woman of some importance was a delicate and risky undertaking. Did she realize what she was asking him to do?

With a grunt of frustration, Phillip brushed back his hair and slipped on a pair of soft and worn moccasins. It was dark out, and a stroll around the dwellings would not be unusual. Rather than walk to the taverns or join a game of cards at another cabin, he would continue around the fringes of the settlement until he picked up the footpath and worked his way through the darkness to the don's abode. He should know the way by heart by now.

The air felt cool against his skin when Phillip stepped outside. Without a waistcoat or jacket, he was dressed quite comfortably for a late evening. He hoped he did not run into the guard, much less Hidalgo or Baca.

Phillip moved as careful along the game trail as possible watching for guards from the fort. When he crept up to the don's garden gate, he found the courtyard empty in the moonlight. He scanned the upstairs windows and saw they were dark but did not dare throw any rocks. He had no idea whose room was whose. Should he wake the wrong Montego, he could be shot.

Phillip dawdled at the gate then reached into his pocket and pulled out a russet and yellow-striped shell he'd found. It was shaped like a tulip flower. He set it gently on the ground beside the post and backed away.

"Is that for me?"

The words spoken from behind him made him yank a small dirk from a sheath at his waist. A soft chuckle came from the trees, and he locked his lips together to keep from growling. She had surprised him this time. Miss Montego stepped out of the shadows.

"I didn't know if you expected me," she confessed. "I thought you might so I slipped out to wait for a while."

"To swim or collect shells?"

She stepped into a puddle of moonlight, and he could see her hair was down and her dressing gown wrapped tight around her waist. "I don't dare go down to the shore again," she said with a pout, "not with pirates and *guardacostas* lurking about."

Phillip glanced toward the house and seeing no one, put a hand on her elbow and urged her a few steps down the path. "Well then, I'll walk with you," he told her, but she hesitated. He gently wrapped his fingers above her wrist like he was all the protection she needed, and she relaxed. They strode under the cover of the trees over damp sand strewn with glowing pebbles.

"I was surprised to see you with Captain Gonzalez," he observed in a stern voice.

"I was surprised to see you at all." Emma stopped. "I thought we had a deal. You said you would kidnap me and take me to Charleston."

Even though she could not see him, Phillip rolled his eyes in the dark. "It can't be done right away."

"I've only a week left," she explained in a nervous tone, "and you left the settlement. How did I know if you'd be back?"

"My comings and goings are none of your business," dictated Phillip. He heard her sharp intake of breath.

"You have no problem making my comings and goings your business," she retorted in a frustrated voice.

"You should not be coming and going anywhere," argued Phillip, "especially with Captain Gonzalez. It's dangerous."

"I haven't told him a thing," insisted Miss Montego. "Why would I?"

Phillip assumed she meant because she could keep a secret. A dangerous one. They walked arm in arm down to the beach as Phillip explained in hushed tones he had come up with a plan. "It shouldn't be too difficult," he hoped.

He held her back for a moment and searched the last bend in the tree line that shielded them from the sight of the fort. "You should not have wandered out into the night all alone," he chided her.

"They make such a racket doing their rounds, how can I not hear them coming?" Miss Montego slipped off her shoes and padded across the sand.

Phillip envied her comfort and ease. He was tempted to take off his moccasins and sink his feet into the gritty coolness, too, but he followed her instead. "You never heard me coming," he pointed out.

Her teeth glimmered in the darkness along with a smile. "I wasn't expecting you, and you were much quieter." She waded into the shallow end of the gentle swishing tide and bent down to pick up a large chunk of a shell. Holding it near her eyes, she said, "This looks very nice."

"It's broken. Why do you always make a beeline for the surf?" he wondered in an amused tone. "There's plenty of shells and driftwood further up on the shore." A blustery breeze rolled off of a group of inbound breakers. It sent her hair trailing behind her in the air like a kite's tail.

"The best ones are where the tide leaves them," she answered, "and I don't mind broken things. They're still beautiful."

Phillip strolled along beside her with shells crunching under his feet. He only stopped when she did and picked through them like she was in a vegetable garden. "Why do you do it, anyway? They're everywhere. Don't they have shells in Charleston?"

"Yes, but not like here. Most of them there are white and small, leftover from the oysters, you see. The best are out on the islands."

"I never paid much attention, I admit." Phillip reached out and touched the collection of shell bits in her upturned hand.

"Have you been to Charleston?" Miss Montego asked.

"Only once," he admitted. "I grew up in Savannah, you recall, and lived there until the war."

She studied him in the darkness. "How did you get to the Indies?"

"I was kidnapped by British forces and forced to sail aboard a man-o-war."

He saw her brows raise in surprise. "During the war?"

"Yes."

"You fought on the other side?" It sounded more like a question than an accusation, but it still stung. "I had no choice," Phillip replied in a steely voice. "I was a child, only ten-years-old."

Emma put a hand to her heart. "Oh, my. I'm so sorry, Mr. Oakley. I didn't know."

"Not many do," he muttered and bent to pretend to look for shells, too.

"Do you miss your family?"

"Much like you, Miss Montego, I have none. They died."

"I'm sorry, Mr. Oakley." After a pause staring into the night, Miss Montego asked, "Is that why you're a pirate then?"

"Indeed." Phillip picked up a handful of sand and let it stream through his fingers. "The British took my family away. I had nothing, and so I take back what I can."

She edged further into the surf until the water touched her hem. "That sounds like quite the grudge."

"It sets things to rights."

"How?" she wondered. "I think anger and revenge is a waste of time. Look at me," she suggested. "I'm not angry that my mama died. I don't blame Don Marcos for leaving me with the family who raised me. I'm certain most people do the best they can, even if they're British," she teased.

"You wouldn't understand, Miss Montego." Phillip admired her good heart despite her ignorance.

She sniffed and returned to his side. "Well, someday your vengeance may cost you your life or the life of someone you care about. If I were you, I'd use the *Revenge* to trade and to travel and to leave the past behind me."

"Is that what you've done? Then why not go to Spain?"

"Because it doesn't feel right, and my past is the only place left for me." Miss Montego sighed. "I wish I could stay here, I do." Her voice quavered with the last of her words.

Phillip dropped down into the sand and sat cross-legged. He studied the moon's path along the water. "The shells are all crushed up here," he complained. "You're lucky to find any good ones."

To his surprise, Miss Montego crouched down beside him. "As long as they're colorful and have a pleasing form, I don't mind if they have a few missing pieces."

"Why not?" Phillip gazed at her curiously. "I wouldn't think they'd make much of a collection."

The woman peered into his eyes through the moonlight. The shushing of the gentle waves made him want to take her hand and lay down beside her in the sand. She gave a sheepish chuckle, and he wondered if she could guess his thoughts.

"I like broken seashells, Mr. Oakley, because it means they've lived a full life—sometimes, perhaps a dangerous life, and the sea has carried them to far off places before bringing them here. They've been tossed and pounded, thrown hither and thither, but at last they've reached these shores, and they can find rest." She fiddled with a piece of shell in her hand. "I pick them up because despite what they've been through, they're still as beautiful and strong as ever."

Phillip touched the shell in her fingers. "That's a very good reason," he admitted in a thick voice. She let it go, and he held it up. It glowed white in the moonlight, but he could see bands across its back although he could not tell its color. "It looks like angel wings," he murmured.

"Perhaps it watched over other seashells," she joked.

He slipped it into his pocket. "I will keep this if you don't mind."

"I don't." She crawled to her feet. Phillip joined her, and they walked further down the shore with eyes searching the sand. Once, their hands brushed, and Phillip resisted the urge to reach out and hold hers. Surely she would think him too bold and pull away.

"Will you take your shells with you to Charleston?" he queried.

"It depends. I am only allowed two trunks according to Captain Gonzalez."

Phillip wrinkled his brow. "Why should he decide what you may or may not take?"

"He's the one who will take me away from here."

"In the *León*?" Phillip exclaimed.

"Yes." Miss Montego eyed him with concern. "Why?"

Phillip put his fingers to his eyelids and pressed them tight. "My dear," he muttered with a sinking heart, "you didn't tell me you would depart on the *León*. I assumed you would go on a merchantman."

"Does it matter?"

Phillip shook himself from the spell she'd cast over him. "It's a Spanish ship, Emma." He clutched his head and tried to control his tongue. "I'm sorry. I meant Miss Montego."

Emma raised her shoulders as if his address was not important. "From what I understand, you've attacked them before."

Phillip raised his hands to take her by the arms, and she jumped back as if afraid of him. "What? Do you think I would strike you?" Offended, he stalked a few steps ahead of her.

"I have no idea, *Phillip*." Her voice quavered. She glowed like a fairy.

"I would never lay a hand on a woman," he retorted, "much less attack a *guardacosta*." A strained silence fell between them broken only by the waves swishing on the shore.

"What do you mean?" she asked in a small voice.

"A merchantman, yes," Phillip explained, struggling for patience, "but now you tell me I am to attack the Spanish Navy?"

She stared, her dark silent eyes boring holes through him.

"Emma," he stuttered, aware he spoke improperly but didn't care, "I put my men and self at risk every time we hoist the black flag, but we take that risk knowing there will be no harm done and a great reward."

"One of these days," she replied in a flat tone, "one of those risks will rise up and fight back. Then you'll be more than a buccaneer, you'll be a real pirate. A murderer. Not just a thief who—"

"Thief?" Phillip threw up his hands. "What do you know about it."

"I know you stop ships under threat of cannon fire and rob them blind," she shot back.

He bit his lip. She was right. Why did it offend his sensibilities then? "Fine," he agreed, "I rob a few ships now and then, but most of my take goes to people who need it—who are in great need."

Emma crossed her arms over her dressing gown as the breeze rippled it like a ship's pennant. He stepped closer, wanting her to understand. "We take little risk for great reward and trade with those along the coast and some of the islands who have next to nothing." He waved his arm about. "The British, the Spanish, the French, and the Dutch, too, are plowing up the New World like teams of careless oxen. They destroy families, livelihoods, and innocent lives."

"Are we so much better in the colonies? Does our government not do the same thing?"

"In a manner of speaking." Phillip thought of his Creek friends and knew that she was right.

She tilted her head at him. "You know it's true, and I've heard that you are very rich; you have a great house in Kingston and many ships, too."

"Fishing boats. I help myself. What else is there for me, and how do you know it?"

"I heard Señor Hidalgo speaking with the don."

Phillip grimaced. "He talks too much."

Emma shrugged. "He admires you. He wants to be a rich, powerful man, too."

"I'm not powerful." Phillip shook his head. "I just – I just—"

"What?" Her brows furrowed in the dim light. "Why do you do it? For retribution? I don't believe it, and how is it any worse than helping me escape?"

He bowed his head and stared at the sand that glowed blue-white under his feet. Why, indeed? To save the poor? Entertain wild and restless men and fill his coffers? He jerked his head up. "Until you've heard the cries of your family and neighbors pleading for mercy, and watched your home burn to the ground, you will never understand."

"The *Revenge*," she whispered. "Is that really all you care about, revenge?"

Phillip realized she understood more than he'd meant for her to know. "I cannot fulfill my end of the bargain, Emma," he whispered. He shuddered at the sound of her betrayed gasp. "Not for revenge or as a heroic deed. I cannot attack a fully loaded battleship in a vessel my size and gamble the lives of innocent men who trust me to sail smart and safe."

"But—"

"There's nothing in it for them," he insisted in a raised tone. "I may get my hands on you, but they'd earn nothing for the risk unless you have a great deal of money hidden in your seashell collection, and that's if they survived."

He saw her jaw tighten in the darkness. "We had a deal, *Phillip*."

"It's impossible!"

She backed away, startled. Shells trickled from her fingers and rattled onto the ground. "You said you'd need something in exchange. I have information." Her voice cracked. "Captain Gonzalez told me all about his ship. I know the weight and how many cannons she carries."

"So do I. There is nothing to be done," Phillip whispered in a gentler tone. "I'm sorry." It felt like his heart fell with a thud to his feet. He could almost feel it tangle around his legs.

He'd looked forward to the scheme more than he'd admitted. The excitement and fun of it, with thoughts of spending time alone with her at sea until they reached Kingston. In the back of his mind, Phillip had considered that she might see his home there and hide away with him until it was safe to make passage to South Carolina.

He'd been a fool. Catching her in the moonlight like a sea nymph and learning she was the daughter of Don Marcos had tantalized him like legends passed around the table with the rum. But this was no story. It would only end in tragedy for him and everyone else, perhaps even Queenie.

"Surely there is something you or your men could do," Emma pleaded. "I have a gold bracelet. Real gold. You can have it."

Phillip cringed. It felt like a blade to the ribs. A band of clouds passed over the moon, and the beach darkened until it was as black as pitch. Queenie had been right. He was in over his head in this dark deal and there was nowhere to escape.

He stepped toward the trees hoping the moon stayed hidden behind the clouds. "I'm sorry. No. Go to Don Marcos if you must, or even Captain Gonzalez, accuse me of pirating, but I will not sacrifice the lives of innocent people I know to save myself—or a young woman as beautiful as you."

"Phillip!" she cried, and he winced, hoping it did not carry on the wind.

"I'm sorry, Emma."

"But I—" Her voice cracked with panicked grief.

"They are all the family I have. Our deal is off." Phillip managed to keep his tone firm. "All of it. Off."

"Well then," she sputtered, "I hope you are caught and dragged up the Thames to the gibbets!" Before she starting throwing seashells like cannonballs, Phillip hurried to disappear into the trees. He strode purposely back to his cabin with a throbbing heart. He could not return to the bayou or camp because it might expose Queenie or the crew of the *Revenge*. Instead, he redressed in a proper waistcoat and coat then burned any incriminating evidence in the event he was arrested by the guard.

EMMA RAN UNTIL SHE felt stabbing pains in her side. When she reached the courtyard gate, she wrapped her arms around it to hold herself up while she heaved for air. Even the cool night could not prevent her from feeling hot all over. The back of her neck felt damp.

Gasping, she rewrapped her gown around herself. The screaming panic in her chest she'd held back erupted as a loud sob, and she pressed her hand over her mouth. Her only hope. Her last chance. Tears raced to fill her eyes. They spilled over and ran down her cheeks.

Why had he said he would do it at all? She should have reported him and shared her suspicions from the beginning. Surely Captain Gonzalez would call again. Did Phillip truly not care if she turned him in?

Straightening, Emma gave one last whimper. She wiped her cheeks with both hands. There was no way to avoid going to Spain unless she ran away, but where to go? The settlement was surrounded by different tribes, some friendly and some not. Beyond their camps laid Spanish-controlled Louisiana. Her throat spasmed, but Emma reigned in her despair so as not to wake the household. She could flat refuse to board, but knowing Don Marcos he would order one of his manservants to drag her onto the ship. She'd never have the nerve to defy him. She had too much respect.

Emma plodded across the yard and slipped into the silent house. The stairs creaked as she crept up them, and she hoped she didn't wake anyone. Moving through the dark like a prowling cat, she turned the knob on the door to her room and slipped inside.

"Where have you been?" whispered a voice in the darkness.

Emma gasped. The silhouette of Roseline sat on the edge of the bed.

"I – I went for a walk." She spoke as quietly as she could.

"In the middle of the night?" Roseline sounded amazed. "Did you leave the courtyard? I looked for you in the garden. Emma! What were you thinking? Who were you with?"

"Why do you think I was with someone?" Emma returned in a hushed tone. She stood frozen in the middle of the room.

Roseline's shadow rose and crossed the room until they could see one another from the light streaming through the window. She took Emma's hand. "Betsy mentioned you were in the courtyard before dawn last week, and tonight, I thought I heard you leave your room, and you didn't come back. I've waited and waited."

"I'm sorry, Roseline." Emma's voice trembled. "I didn't mean to frighten you or keep you awake."

Roseline pressed Emma's fingers with her soft hand. "Is it Captain Gonzalez? Has he encouraged you to meet with him?"

Emma felt her face crumple with offense and even a little distaste. "No. That's not it at all."

"Then tell me you have just been out of the gate for good reason."

Emma could not lie, but she didn't know if Roseline could be trusted with the truth. She always did the right thing and never complained. She found happiness in her station in life without wanting something more or different."

"It's my shells," said Emma in a weak voice.

"Shells?"

"Yes, and..." Emma took a deep breath and pulled her to the bed to sit down close together. "I told you I cannot go to Spain. I can't bear it. I was trying to find a way out of it."

She heard Roseline swallow. "Darling, what have you done?"

Emma wrapped her arms around her. "I'm sorry. I cannot tell you. It might get someone into trouble, but you must trust me. Please."

"Then what do you plan to do?"

"Nothing," Emma sniffled. "I failed. I could not save myself even when I tried."

"Please don't tell me you've left in the middle of the night before."

"I have," admitted Emma in a soft voice, "but always alone and only to find special seashells."

Roseline groaned.

"No, it's safe. I stay in the shadows of the footpath and make sure no one is about. Sometimes I go to cool off, to be alone, or to watch the turtles come up on the beach. I just want to feel free."

"You are free here," Roseline scolded in a stern tone.

Emma wondered desperately how to make her understand. "As much as I've grown to love it, you must know the hacienda feels like a prison sometimes. Everything is so proper and orderly, and I cannot leave the yard without an escort. It can be unbearable."

"Darling, it is for your safety. This is not your city off the river. There is no protection except for the fort and the few ships in the harbor."

"I've never come to any harm," Emma promised in a desperate voice. "Please, don't tell the don. If anything, help me find a way to escape going to Spain."

"Escape? Why would you not want to go, Emma? I know you have concerns, but it's nothing to fear."

"No, Roseline, not concerns. I can't go. I won't. There is nothing and no one for me there, and I will never fit in."

"Why ever not?" Roseline sounded confused. "I would love to take your place."

"Then do. Go," Emma offered with bitterness. "If I cannot stay in Pensacola, I wish only to return to the land that I know."

"But what would you do?"

Emma sat back with a gutted sigh. "I could find a situation and be independent, or marry—someday."

"That is why you must go to Spain," urged Roseline.

"There are plenty of men here," insisted Emma. "Quite a lot, and more than females. I know Don Marcos wishes me to make an aristocratic match, but I don't care about that."

"What about a certain gentleman here now?" Roseline asked carefully.

"Please do not say Captain Gonzalez," moaned Emma. "He is amiable and a good captain, I'm sure, but I don't think I could love him."

Roseline curled her leg up on the bed. The soft rustle of her robe slid across the thin linen blanket. "Tell me then, Emma, if you *had* to choose, who would you choose in Pensacola?"

"What?"

"If the don allowed you to choose for yourself—anyone—and you had to make a choice, who would you choose?"

Phillip Oakley shot straight to her lips, but Emma clamped her jaws shut before he could escape. She swallowed his name down. "Oh, Roseline. Maybe there would be someone, but why does it matter?"

Roseline leaned forward. "If you are so desperate to stay you are leaving the hacienda at night then perhaps I should help you. Promise me first that you are not thinking of running away."

Emma wanted to lie down in Roseline's lap and cry and tell her everything. How could Phillip Oakley let her down? She almost banged her fists on the bed.

"Emma?"

Her eyes watered despite her every effort to keep tears at bay.

"What is it?" whispered Roseline. She sat as still as a statue.

"I thought I had a plan," Emma divulged after a painful pause. "Oh, Roseline," she whispered in agony. "It was all worked out, but now it's fallen apart."

Her companion embraced her, and Emma cried silently for a few minutes. "If you want to stay in Pensacola, we will find a way," Roseline promised her.

Raising her head, Emma peered at her to measure her sincerity. "Do you mean it?"

"I do," Roseline whispered. "It will break the don's heart, for he loves you and wants what's best for you although you do not believe it." She let out a small sigh. "The truth is, Emma, he is ill, more than you know. The time is not far distant that you will be an orphan again, and that is why he wishes you to go to Spain."

"He's going to... die?"

Roseline made a soft noise of comfort. "We all will someday. His time is not that far distant is all."

Despite the news and all that it meant, Emma's heart sank. Nausea unfurled in her stomach. "So whether I go or stay, he will pass."

Roseline nodded in the darkness. "Very soon."

CHAPTER NINE

Phillip stayed up two nights before he surrendered to sleep. Eventually, the heat of the day made it impossible to rest any longer. He washed his face with tepid water from the pitcher beside his bed, and a loud knock startled him. With a deep breath, he strode across the cabin floor to answer it. It was not guards, but a small boy with bear grease-slicked hair. He held up a crushed piece of parchment, and Phillip offered a coin in exchange.

With a sigh of relief, he wasted no time unfolding it. In Chekilli's neat handwriting, Phillip read that the pelts were ready, and he could pick them up at the northwest trail crossing that branched toward the Creek's lands in one direction and into the bayou in the other.

Phillip returned to his room to finish dressing. He expected the *Mary Alice* to return any day and would watch for her while keeping an eye on the fort should a soldier—or a certain naval captain—come looking for him.

He had no reason to dislike Gonzalez but many for avoiding him. True, something else bothered Phillip although he'd tried to deny it. The officer of notable family had taken it upon himself to befriend the don, cozy up to the governor, and behave in an overly-attentive way toward Emma. To heap insult onto injury, the Spaniard had called on her and taken her for a turn around Pensacola like it was some kind of English garden.

Phillip ground his teeth and grabbed his haversack and long musket. He would like nothing better than to snatch Emma from her bed. With a wistful smirk, he marched outside and waved to his close neighbors to make sure they knew he was off to buy pelts to ship out of Pensacola. It looked a great deal more legal than scuttling about to avoid accusations of piracy.

So far, it appeared Emma had said nothing, but time would tell. It would be best, he supposed, if he never returned to the port, not until the don whisked her away on her voyage across the sea to *España*.

A heavy feeling much like a fishing weight hung on him. There was no reason for him to be alarmed at how distraught Emma looked when he informed her the deal was off. He'd done the right thing. He would never compromise the lives of his friends. There was no other choice.

The long walk to the wilderness crossing took until night-fall. Phillip found Chekilli waiting there with four men, three rickety wagons, and several horses. He greeted them politely in their language and settled at a small campfire apart from them to rest.

The hunters seemed genuine. He'd paid them in Spanish coin from money exchanged at the treasury, surprised they did not ask for guns. Perhaps they had a supplier elsewhere, he reasoned, for weapons were the true currency of the Florida frontier. Had Chekilli not been there and vouched for their honor, Phillip would have set off right away. As it was, he chose to sleep and trust the two hired drivers would be there in the morning to help him return the tall stack of skins to the settlement.

Conversations under the low, grasping oaks sprawled across the ground began to diminish with the buzzing of insects and flapping of wings. Phillip stirred the ashes of his fire miserably.

"You are unhappy."

Phillip looked up as Chekilli crouched across from him. He dropped a blackened stick to the ground.

"Not with our business. It was a good deal."

His partner lifted his chin in agreement. "Once we go our separate ways, I return to the camp."

"Yes, about that," Phillip warned. "It seems yet again Miss Montego has upset the apple cart."

Chekilli raised his eyes but otherwise remained impassive as if he'd expected it.

Phillip drew a breath of courage. "The ship her papa has arranged for her to travel to Havana aboard is the *León*."

The corners of Chekilli's mouth slipped into a frown. Before he could speak, Phillip raised a hand to stop him. "I know. It's impossible."

"An invitation to slice us like cheese."

"I told her so," Phillip related. "The deal is off."

After musing over this and finding it satisfactory, Chekilli inquired, "How do you know she will not reveal you? They will come searching for us."

Phillip exhaled with fatigue. "I don't know. That is my expectation, which is why I remained for a few days but nothing happened. The widow and neighbors know I have come to pick up my pelts. Perhaps I will be arrested when I return. That is why you must only take me as far as you feel it is safe to go. The drivers can continue since they have alibis. You should return to camp as planned, and if I am not detained once the *Mary Alice* is on her way, I'll meet you at the usual place, board *Revenge*, and we'll set off for the Indies."

"I agree," said Chekilli in a soft voice. "There is no reason to loiter in these waters."

"Not if she gives me up. Billy will have his hands full proving his innocence and protecting the *Mary Alice*, but it's my intention to have him give me up should it come to that."

"Just you?"

Phillip nodded. "I've lain awake the past few nights trying to sort it out. I'll make sure the *Revenge* is spotted without you or anyone else aboard. Everyone will have to go their separate ways. Perhaps Nassau. Or Tobago."

Chekilli frowned. "I would stay here in the bayou. There is nothing for me out there, and I have no wish to be captured in Kingston without papers."

"Of course." Phillip knew his friend had no protection from being kidnapped and forced into bondage, no matter how elegant his English and penmanship. His dark eyes, dark hair, and mother's Creek blood kept him no safer than a pirate on the Thames. It was better to stay on Spanish soil in the recesses of uninhabited swamps. "Until then," continued Phillip, "I will lay low in my humble abode until *Mary Alice* arrives. Time will tell."

"*Cehecarēs.* I will see you later then, I hope."

Phillip dropped his gaze back to the red-orange ashes.

"Perhaps you will have the opportunity to bring more than supplies to the camp."

As Chekilli raised himself off of the ground with little effort, Phillip stopped him. "What do you mean?"

"Why must you kidnap the woman from a ship?"

Phillip blinked. "Because her father's house is a fortress."

"Not in the middle of the night when the tide is out."

"Yes," Phillip agreed, "but I can't pilfer her from the beach in her nightdress. They will search for her—and might be drawn to the bayou."

"The *Revenge* could sail out before then."

"What about Queenie and others?"

His friend paused then allowed a forlorn look. "You are right, Phillip. It's too dangerous. The only way for Miss Montego to avoid going to Spain is to escape the *León* in plain sight."

"You're right, and she must stand up to Don Marcos and do it on her own."

EMMA SAT IN THE SMALL stone church staring up at a crucifix and trying not to think of the morrow. Roseline reached over to hold her hand to comfort her. They had not come up with a plan. Roseline could only suggest that perhaps a union with Captain Gonzalez would not be unbearable, and she could beg to stay in Pensacola.

The murmur of the congregation roused Emma from her desperate reflections, and she squeezed her rosary. Through her veil, she felt certain no one could see the panic she felt. Every slant of the sun from a different angle made her pulse quicken. Time was short, and yet in the back of her mind, she knew if worse came to worse, she could always run away in Havana.

The prayers finally ended, and she stood meekly to follow the don out. He glanced back at her once, and an expression of satisfaction flashed in his eyes.

"You look lovely this morning," he observed as they walked out into the damp heat. "Isn't the weather fair?" He glanced across the bay, and as if called by some unspoken arrangement, Captain Gonzalez appeared in the sunlight.

Emma stepped back in surprise.

"Ah, Captain!" declared Don Marcos. They spoke together in low murmurs while Emma hovered under a parasol. She looked across the water. A jumble of boats and small ships danced over gentle swells in the harbor. A tall three-masted ship entered and glided inland. Emma squinted her eyes. It was the *Mary Alice*. Phillip's ship had returned a third time. Would he board now? The bitter betrayal she'd staggered under for days pitched up in her throat. Her initial horror had brewed into anger and her anger into a hunger for revenge.

The scoundrel! The pirate! He'd never had any intention of rescuing her from being forced across the sea. Like a silver-tongued devil, he'd told her everything she wanted to hear and made all of the proper assurances while never having any intention of carrying it out. With eyes on his merchantman, Emma's knee twitched as she restrained herself from stomping her foot. He would no doubt make an appearance at the most convenient time. She had not seen him since he'd backed out of the deal.

"What is it?"

Emma jumped at the sound of Roseline's voice in her ear. "It's nothing," she assured her but was unable to withhold the bitterness from her tone.

Beside her with her veil lifting and falling in the pleasant salty breeze, Roseline looked out across the water. "The *Mary Alice*. Mr. Oakley's ship has returned."

"Yes," acknowledged Emma in a tight voice, "and I hope she carries him out again real soon and for good."

Roseline stared at her with undisguised curiosity. Through her thin shroud, Emma shifted her eyes so their gazes did not meet. Even a veil could not hide the trembling she felt every time she thought of Phillip, and for all the wrong reasons!

"Señorita?" She spun at the sound of Captain Gonzalez's voice. "I trust you are well this morning and prepared for our journey tomorrow."

Emma gave a small dip at the knee. "Yes, and I thank you for your concern."

"She is in good health," Roseline assured him. "We are both looking forward to the voyage."

"And you will stay in Havana for a time I understand," approved the captain.

Roseline glanced at Emma. "Just for a short time to visit my brother and his family and then I will return."

He raised his chin like he already knew it. The don looked pleased like he was close to finishing a long-awaited plan. Emma realized he could not wait to be rid of her. She reached out without thinking, and the captain caught her arm.

"Would you like to walk, Señorita Montego?" he assumed then turned to the don for permission. Before she knew it, they were strolling down the sandy avenue with Captain Gonzalez explaining the boarding procedures the next morning. Try as she might, Emma could not pay attention, for the *Mary Alice* was sliding past the docks where she would be reined in and tied off.

"Ah, see," noticed Captain Gonzalez following her gaze, "Señor Oakley's ship is in."

Despite the pin that pricked her heart, Emma remarked, "I suppose that means he will be on his way again." *And good riddance.*

"Yes," agreed the captain gazing at the streaming pennant. "Odd he does not join her on some of her trips further up the coast."

Concern washed over Emma. Despite her fury at Phillip's betrayal, she did not want him to be caught. "He had trade with the hunters who live outside of the settlement. I understand he deals in a great many pelts."

"Sí. That is all they have to offer in this God-forsaken place."

Emma glanced sideways at him.

"Forgive me," he amended. "I am missing home."

Emma couldn't believe he thought such a thing of this beautiful place. "You did not enjoy your time here in Pensacola?"

He offered her a genuine smile. "There were some aspects," he admitted, "such as your company when I was in port, Señorita Montego, but no, I do not love my post here in West Florida and am happy to be returning to Havana even if it is for a short time."

Emma chewed her lip hoping he could not see her through the veil. "And where will the *León* sail after Havana?"

"I'm not certain. It is likely I will return here to the harbor although it may be up the other coastline to St. Augustine."

"How much you do wander," she remarked, "for as much as you wish to return to Spain."

A soft smile touched the corners of his mouth, and they began to walk again around the outside walls of the fort. "Perhaps I will return to Spain with you, Emma," he suggested in a gentle voice.

She inhaled sharply. Did he have an inkling of her intentions? Honesty fell from her lips, she could not help herself. "I do not wish to go to Spain, Captain Gonzalez," she confided. "I love it here, and I wish to stay."

He looked at her with surprise. "But you will love it there."

"I don't wish to love it," she mumbled.

He chuckled as if she told a joke, and she realized she'd spoken dangerously. "See Señorita Montego, you are a rare gem and wield a great family name. You will join me on the *León* in the morning, and by Havana, I promise you will feel differently."

Emma bit her lip. There was no use in arguing. She might as well be speaking to Don Marcos. Roseline's idea for Emma to hint to Captain Gonzales that she would marry him if she could stay in Pensacola looked hopeless. He thought of her as nothing more than a pretty object as flattering as it was, but just like the don, he did not want her to stay in Pensacola, either.

EMMA RODE IN SILENCE. The gilded carriage, a rarity in Pensacola, rolled smoothly over the sandy road to the harbor. Leading the way was the don astride one of his fine stallions. A wagon heaped with trunks trudged along behind the carriage at the end of their parade. Shopkeepers stepped out of their shop doors and waved their handkerchiefs in the air. Roseline nodded at them in approval so she did not tear up. For Roseline's sake, Emma remained stoic.

As they approached the harbor, gulls circled overhead like sharks and waited for scraps of fish from the fishermen's gutted catches. The breeze smelled of fish and tar. Emma wrinkled her nose.

"See now," whispered Roseline, "we still have a week ahead of us to share with Captain Gonzalez." She took a shaky but confident breath. "Don't worry, Emma, we shall sort it out."

They would not. It was too late. Emma felt it was time to make her understand. "He will not do, Roseline. I mentioned my preference to stay here on our stroll yesterday morning, and he laughed at me and ignored it completely."

"He may feel differently after spending more time with you. Women hold persuasive power over most men," she winked. "I don't have to chaperone your every moment."

Emma huffed at the very idea of betraying her dignity. Her traveling gown felt loose and comfortable, but Betsy had laced her so tight in her stays her ribs were crushed. "He doesn't like Pensacola, he can't wait to leave it. Besides, I could never betray him like—" She caught herself. *Like Phillip Oakley betrayed me.* "You asked if I tossed and turned throughout the night, and I did, but it is not because I have any machinations of capturing the captain's heart—at least not that one," she added in a bitter tone.

Roseline gave her a steady stare that spun with questions. "Is there another captain? There is someone, isn't there?"

Emma couldn't help but glance at the *Mary Alice* becalmed on the water. Roseline followed her gaze. After a weighted pause, Roseline warned, "Captain Gonzalez is a good man, and there are few other options." She sighed. "I wish you would have told me of your determination sooner."

"I did," cried Emma in a strangled voice, "but you would not listen. No one listens!"

"I'm sorry, Emma," choked Roseline. "Like your father, I only want what's best for you."

Emma gave a dry, forced laugh. "Don Marcos does not want me here. It's as if all of Pensacola can't wait for me to leave."

"Now, now," soothed Roseline. "Let us be determined to have a fine time of it, and we'll sort it all out when we get to Havana. There are single men there, too, and more captains, as well."

Emma shuddered. This was not how she ever imagined choosing someone to wed. "I do wish I'd been kidnapped by pirates," she mumbled as the carriage drew up to a stop.

Roseline gasped then gave a nervous chuckle. "Don't be silly, my sweet. That would be a fate worse than death." The *León* loomed overhead, swaying back and forth on the water.

So be it, thought Emma. Death could not be as awful as living all alone in a foreign land.

CHAPTER TEN

Phillip packed up the cabin and sent his trunk ahead. He was dressed like a gentleman—the wealthy trader he was reputed to be. How long would it last if people knew he was an orphaned farm boy who'd grappled his way out of poverty and up the ladders of society? No one in the New World asked questions when coins trickled through your fingers. Until they caught you pirating, that is.

He borrowed a horse for a small fee and trotted toward the harbor as the morning sun crested and turned the world golden. There was a smart breeze which meant good sailing, and he was glad. He yearned for the cooler winds that swept across the sea rather than the fastidious gusts across Pensacola. It was time to escape his obsession with Emma Montego. She would never have him, and he would never have her unless he abducted her. Such was the irony.

Queenie would expect to see him one last time, he suspected, to put her mind at ease. Rubbing his lips together, Phillip hoped there would be time. Billy would sail him out of the harbor as usual and drop him off on the cay southeast of the bayou. From there, he would slip off into the mire and round up the crew. They'd laid low during the first half of the horrible summer heat, but now most welcomed getting back to sea and pirating even with the sky blazing at midday. They would slink into their hidden cove on Jamaica by night, and Chekil-li would take command and set off for Tobago or one of their other haunts leaving Phillip in Kingston. He would live as a rich merchant, or the pirate hunters would catch up with him if Emma spilled his secrets.

He grunted. The logistics of it all made him tired. He'd gone to extraordinary lengths to have his revenge on life and fate—and to get rich, but besides the company of the crew when they refitted in beautiful places and were free to relax, it brought him little pleasure now.

The towering masts of harbor ships rose before him, and Phillip climbed down and passed the horse off to a tavern's stable boy. Down the quay alongside the *León* and her seamen in dark, uncomfortable garb, Phillip eyed a fine carriage he recognized as belonging to Don Marcos. He could not take his eyes from it as he walked along.

Don Marcos stood in the shadows of the ship. Phillip watched him bid farewell to his daughter with a few words and a formal bow, and his heart wilted. She seemed one to throw her arms around her parents and embrace them fiercely, he thought. It was odd the man would send her away, but he was aged and frail. Perhaps it was best he turned over his daughter to the Montego family after all.

Phillip caught a glimpse of Emma's face as she marched up the gangplank. She looked like she was about to face a firing squad. His heart went out to her in all directions. She was a true Spanish beauty, yet she had the same spirit his American family, friends, and neighbors had carried in their hearts in that place that had once been home. How she reminded him of the quiet, simple, and diverting life in Savannah. It was no wonder she yearned to return to Charleston.

Phillip studied her long regal neck and saw her shoulders squared. They'd both been born into freedom no matter which country claimed them as property now, he mused. He reached into his pocket and rubbed the seashell that he'd kept from the last night they'd walked and talked together.

Yes, he was a broken shell of a man. He had no family and no country, yet he'd seen much of the world and traveled near and far. He was chipped, but he was strong. The mystery was, why had he washed up on Pensacola's shores?

An ache to be settled and quietly content washed over him. Phillip felt his shoulders slump from the disappointment of what could have been with Emma. She'd kept his secret although he'd pulled out of their deal. He'd betrayed her and let her down. Surely she understood. If she could only know Queenie and Chekilli and what it would cost...

What kind of girl would not be a burden in the bayou? A girl who'd lived in the Carolina low country, that's who. A girl who did not faint at the mention of snakes and alligators. A girl who did not think twice about taking a walk in the moonlight. A girl who would defend herself even if she was outmatched. And most impressively, a girl who understood freedom and independence and would sacrifice fine gowns and fine living just to have them.

A lump swelled in Phillip's throat as he reached the pier where the *Mary Alice* was docked. Captain Gonzalez and the *León* were going to carry away the biggest treasure that had ever sailed into Pensacola.

He stumbled in his ambling gait as he watched Emma's companion walk gracefully up the gangplank beside her. The woman turned her head as if she felt his stare, and he met her clever yellow-brown hawk eyes. He turned sharply away should she see the ravishing admiration he carried for her ward. It was then he noticed how closely docked the *León* and *Mary Alice* were together. Like shy lovers at arm's-length, they bobbed up and down on the morning tide nodding in agreement.

EMMA BOARDED THE HEAVILY-laden gunship and greeted Captain Gonzalez, who Roseline whispered, could not keep his eyes off of her. In her traveling gown and with the don's bracelet clasped around her wrist, Emma stood at the rail beneath a parasol and waved goodbye to the father she still did not know. He didn't wait for the ship to set sail but saluted her one last time and departed on horseback with the empty carriage following him from behind.

"See how sad the carriage looks without us," Emma lamented.

"It will miss you," teased Roseline.

"At least it still has Don Marcos to ferry about."

"Oh my dear, the don purchased that carriage for you and had it delivered before you ever arrived here."

"Did he?" wondered Emma in surprise.

Roseline leaned over the rail and studied the foaming water.

"With you leaving, I'm afraid the carriage will most likely be sold or traded before too long."

The thought of it made Emma sad. She wistfully followed Roseline below deck to their assigned quarters. Emma's space was so tiny she could touch both sides of the bulwark easily while standing in the middle. Poor Roseline, settled next door, did not have a view, so Emma decided to be grateful she had a good-sized porthole although she knew her room would be disassembled and a cannon rolled up to her "window" should the *León* decide to fire its weapons. She stood at the porthole and stared. Several yards away, Phillip's ship swayed back and forth on the water, and she searched the upper deck for him. Would he sail out today, too?

After several long minutes, Emma sat down on her small cot with a sigh. Roseline rapped on the bulwark between them, and she knocked back trying to feel some sort of amusement. She was sure Roseline was already unpacking her things, which meant Emma should do the same before her companion swished in and insisted on doing it for her. They were on their own now, without the luxuries of the hacienda.

There was another knock, but Emma decided it was just a bump. She settled back on the cot and closed her eyes when there was another sound, and it did not come from Roseline's side.

Thunk. There it was again. She looked at the porthole in surprise. Her first thought was that a bird had flown into the side of the ship, but before she could feel sorry for the poor creature, a thick, naked arm appeared in the porthole, and she jumped to her feet. Another arm joined its mate, and Emma stumbled backward with her hand over her mouth. Before she could scream, Phillip Oakley's red face appeared in the center of the hole, his mouth a tight, determined grimace. Emma gasped.

"Well," he grunted between clenched teeth, "how about a little help?"

Emma shot a look at the bulkhead between her and Roseline's room in the event her friend could see through the wall then rushed to the porthole and grabbed hold of Phillip's wet shoulders. Straining with all of her might, she pulled as he scrambled forward and finally slipped through the opening to fall on top of her.

Unable to hold his weight, Emma collapsed onto the floor with a loud smack, landing painfully on her back. Phillip's chest landed on her face, and she let out a muffled groan before she regained her senses and tried to push him off of her. "Get. Off. Me. You great big oaf!"

He rolled off to the side and fell onto his back next to her. Emma caught him looking sideways at her, their noses just inches apart. His face sliced into a giant grin, and he began to laugh under his breath.

Emma sat up with a jerk. "What have you done? Phillip! What are you doing here?"

She looked around her tiny compartment and realized the enormity of the situation. "You can't be here," she hissed. "Have you gone mad? Captain Gonzales has been asking questions about you!"

"Has he?" Phillip sat up across from her and leaned his back against the other bulkhead. "I wondered when he would put two and two together."

Emma looked around the room to regain some sort of composure. "Listen!" she shushed him. The ship trembled as sails were unfurled from the yardarms. The bosun shouted orders, and the vessel lurched.

He waved a hand. "Oh, don't worry yet. They'll have a longboat in the water to tow her out until she can catch her wind."

Emma raised her brows for emphasis and leaned forward. "You can't be here. If they catch you aboard they'll think you're a spy."

"Or a stowaway. Or," Phillip continued, climbing to his feet and peering out of the porthole, "a pirate."

"Yes," she hissed, "a pirate. And you're in my room!"

He stretched his lips into a narrow grin. "You did say you wanted to be kidnapped, didn't you?"

"Yes, but now?" Emma's mind swirled like a hurricane. Captain Redbird had climbed into her quarters through a porthole.

He examined something out of the hole and beckoned her to join him with a curling wave of his hand. Unable to resist, Emma climbed up beside him and peeked outside.

The *León* was just beginning to nudge out of its slip. Phillip pointed across the short span of water to the *Mary Alice*. "Do you see that beam there, and the sheet of canvas dangling in the water?"

"Yes..." Emma's thudding heart stuttered to a stop.

"Brace yourself, and when I give the word, I'm going to slip out and pull you into the water behind me."

"You'll what?"

"They won't see us at all. We'll duck under the water and swim across to the canvas there and hide behind it."

"In the water?"

"What other suggestion do you have? Fly?"

"But—"

"There are no buts and no time," Phillip blurted. "See, we are moving." His body became rigid, and he reached back for her hand.

"But my things!" Emma gazed around the little room. Her trunk sat unopened against the cot. "My clothes. My shells. My money!"

"Money?" Phillip barked in a whisper. "You can't fit that trunk through a porthole, and I'm afraid you'll have to collect new shells. Now, take my hand."

Emma's wide-eyed gaze shot from the trunk to her traveling gown and then back to the porthole. His hand clasped around her wrist.

"Get ready now. You can swim, right?"

"Yes, but Phillip," she hissed, heart pounding like a drum.

From his crouched position, Phillip swung his face and raked her over with his smoldering blue stare. "It's through the porthole or on to Havana, Señorita Montego."

Emma swallowed. The ship bounced, and she saw it move a few more inches past the larboard side of the *Mary Alice*. Dark water swirled around the waterline.

"Ready?"

Emma felt the weight of her world and Phillip's, too, when *Yes* trickled off her tongue. She regretted there would be no time to say goodbye to Roseline the moment her arm jerked forward as Phillip slid through the porthole like a beaver. He dragged her through it behind him. She had no time to arrange herself but plunked out of the opening just as the *León* slipped past the stern of the *Mary Alice*. Together they fell headfirst into salty fizzing water that felt cold at first then became like a warm bath as it bubbled around her. She dare not open her eyes. It would sting, and she'd hardly had time to suck in a mouthful of air.

Phillip pulled her through wet darkness while Emma struggled to kick her legs. She felt her shoes slip off and wondered how long she could survive without air. The weight of her petticoats and gown began to feel leaden like it would drag her down into the depths.

She kicked and struggled, fingers digging into Phillip's hand in desperation as her heart raged against her ribs. Just as she knew she would gasp and scream beneath the water, she felt a jerk, and Phillip's arm went around her waist and pulled her to the surface. She gasped and coughed, eyes blinking and stinging as she looked around. They were hidden behind a long piece of canvas sail draped over the ship's rail. It concealed them from view. The dank boards of the stern swayed dangerously close to their heads.

"Careful," warned Phillip as his other arm reached overhead for a thick rope.

Cloaked behind the sheet of canvas which blocked the sun and view of the departing *León*, Emma felt wet and heavy. She fought to breathe and clung to Phillip like a bur. Fighting to steady her wheezes and not burst into panicked tears, she managed to utter calmly, "Phillip, how long?" and he answered, "Now, Emma," as the line he clung to began to reel them upward.

"Wrap your arms around my neck," he ordered, "but for pity's sake, don't strangle me."

She didn't need to be told twice. Emma wrapped her limbs around him like vines, feeling her bare feet brush against his strong legs below the surface. She clung to his neck and buried her head in his shoulder. He smelled like the sea and something else—something homey and musky and good. Her mouth pressed against the skin of his throat, and she held it there, tasting his warmth and not wanting to be separated from it. It comforted her and yet at the same time, made her body burn with hope and longing. What had become of her?

At last, she felt herself rise from the water but held her eyes shut. After several uncomfortable bumps between the ship's planks and the sour-smelling canvas, Emma felt different arms reach around her waist. She looked in surprise as an officer leaned out of a gun port and pulled her through.

She landed with a thump on a narrow deck with a low ceiling and rows of slender cannons. Phillip wiggled through the hole like a worm and plopped down beside her. Emma looked up at the man who'd helped them. He looked bemused and hurried at the same time. Glancing over his shoulder, he whispered, "We must hurry before someone sees."

Phillip scampered to his bare feet. He waved a finger back and forth between Emma and their champion. "Emma, this is Captain Page if you do not recognize him. Billy, this is the don's Señorita Montego."

The fair young man looked her over with a faint expression of curiosity.

"It's Miss Montego," she blurted as Phillip climbed to his feet.

Seawater ran down his breeches and dripped onto the deck. Emma looked down at her soaked gown. It clung to her skin and framed her sprawled legs in a most unbecoming fashion. She quickly bent them under herself, but Phillip reached for her elbows and pulled her up. The boards felt smooth under her toes. She knew her hair, now all undone, hung heavy and sopping down her back.

"Hurry, Emma," he urged, all business again, and she followed him as he trailed on the heels of the officer who looked for all the world like a commander that knew all of Redbird's secrets.

They hurried across the deck until Captain Page stopped and swung open the door to a small room. Phillip pulled Emma forward and pushed her inside between acrid-smelling barrels and rows of muskets hanging on the walls.

She twisted in surprise. Phillip drew the door almost closed but wedged his face in. "There are blankets and some drink to keep you warm, but you must stay hidden for now."

Emma opened her mouth to protest but no words came out. All she could do was stare, and Phillip dropped his gaze like he was sorry then shut the door with a click and the room fell into darkness.

Emma's heart galloped with angst, and she put her hand across it as seawater streamed down her clothes and hair and skin. It fell with *plipping* sounds onto the decking. Besides ghostly thumps and bumps overhead, the only other sounds she heard was the noise of her breathing. *Good gracious*, she thought. *What have I gotten myself into?*

PHILLIP FOLLOWED BILLY up the ladder and slipped into his own quarters to dry off and change before any of the crew saw him. He knew they would keep Emma a secret, but he couldn't chance a loose tongue.

A strange energy bubbled through his veins. He hadn't felt this much courage or hope in so many years, and why? It was a foolish and risky endeavor. A part of him had thought Emma might not come; that she would surrender to her fate rather than fling herself overboard into the harbor with him. To his relief, she had not panicked or screamed, although he'd felt the fear in her tight grip on his hand. When she'd flung her arms—and legs—around him beneath the cover of the canvas Billy dropped overboard to hide them, he wanted to forget about climbing into the belly of the *Mary Alice* and just cuddle and comfort his hostage.

Just a glimpse of her along the quay had changed everything. He was full of determination to keep his end of the deal despite the unknown dangers. If caught, he knew he would be hung. None of it, however, seemed to matter when considering the alternative. Emma Montego would never be able to say that Phillip Oakley was a coward with no honor.

He admitted he hoped she might say and think and feel vastly different things, although the possibility that they could ever have a future together was out of reach as long as he sailed the *Revenge*. He hoped now she might forgive him in some way for stumbling onto her beach and frightening her near to death, not to mention threatening to expose her midnight swims to the settlement and don in exchange for her silence.

Phillip felt the *Mary Alice* complain and then finally give way as she was nudged out of her resting spot. By the time he strode out of his quarters and through the passage to the deck above, the ship was in the middle of the bay, swaying merrily on the bouncing water as the wind carried her past the protective barrier island where the battery sat too attentive for his liking.

Not too far distant ahead, sailed the *León*. Her flourished stern winked at them as she ducked her head and caught the wind to seek out deeper waters and find her southeasterly course.

How long it would be before they discovered Emma missing, he could not fathom. It was probably her companion who would raise the alarm. The thought of her fear for Emma pricked him with guilt. He wondered if the lady would ever sort out what had happened.

When he joined Billy at the con, the *Mary Alice* was rounding the end of Santa Rosa, a long stretch of grass and sand that protected the mainland from hurricanes and intruders.

"Captain Page." He greeted him with a slight bow, and Billy sent the men around them scurrying away. He motioned for Phillip to join him.

"We managed to get you aboard and hide your cargo undetected, I believe," he observed in a tense tone.

"I'm sorry," murmured Phillip. "It was too easy being moored so closely."

"But the don's daughter?" questioned his friend from the corner of his mouth. "What if we are searched?"

"I'll get down there first and throw her out another porthole."

Billy looked sideways at him and choked down a laugh of disbelief.

"It's the only way," said Phillip with a grimace.

Billy fell silent for a few ship-lengths across the water. "You will give the men a surprise when you're lowered in the skiff at the bayou's river mouth. They assume you have a home there—or a woman."

"Well," mused Phillip with a churlish grin, "now I do. Hopefully, none of them will question how she came aboard. It is better to have no one else involved or informed."

Billy let out a heavy breath and chewed on the side of his lip. Phillip followed his gaze to the men in the ratlines scrambling around like squirrels in the trees.

"The less they know the better," repeated Phillip under his breath.

"Have her wear the disguise I left in the storeroom," Billy urged. "She could be recognized, and word would get out no matter how many oaths are taken."

"You're right, I suspect. I'm moving faster than I can think it through. They may be loyal to our pirating secrets to save their own necks, but they've nothing to do with this."

The captain lifted his chin. "What will you tell the crew of the *Revenge* in the camp?"

"I'm not sure." Phillip hesitated. "I think perhaps I shall take her to Queenie first."

Billy glanced at him with alarm written all over his face.

"I'll leave her there for a time and ready the ship and explain everything to the men. They are anxious to get under sail, but not with a woman aboard. I'll have to make it worth their while in prey and pay."

"And what will you do with her afterward?"

"She wants to return to Charleston. Although there is nothing for her there, I don't see any other recourse."

Billy grunted in agreement. He'd made it clear when Phillip burst into his captain's quarters to tell him of his impulsive plan, that Emma must stay out of sight and only remain on board for as little time as possible. Phillip had agreed, of course, but as to what to do next he was not certain other than to take her to the bayou.

"Queenie will know what to do," he reasoned. He wandered forward and watched the *León* fade away in the distance. He hushed his anxious heart and offered up thanks to anyone listening in the heavens that Emma's absence had not been discovered yet. Surely, the ship would turn about right away and return to Pensacola.

With luck, Phillip reasoned nervously, they would presume she'd somehow fallen overboard. She had, after all, it was just she'd fallen over with him. A mischievous grin tugged at the corner of his mouth. It was not the British, no, but he felt deeply satisfied to have pillaged the don's daughter out from under Gonzalez's nose. Was he jealous of the Spanish captain with the fine family and impressive ship? Yes, Phillip admitted to himself, he was, but Emma had chosen to run away with him.

He watched the long arm of Santa Rosa slide past the ship and eyed the mainland as they hugged the coast. It grew greener and thicker with trees. Anxious and worrying if Emma was frightened in the dark munitions room, he forced himself to wait to check on her until they were within sight of the river mouth. With a last look at Billy, he strode across the deck for the nearest hatch, jumped down the ladder with a thunderous clap to the decking below, and hurried to his room for his haversack and lockbox. He called for the officers' steward, passed him his things, and then as he felt the *Mary Alice* begin to slow her pace, took his time maneuvering to the gun deck as if he had nowhere else to be and was wandering around in idle curiosity.

No one was about when he rapped lightly on the door before unlocking it with Billy's key. He peered into the shadows until Emma stumbled forward into the murky light of the passage squinting at him.

"You changed, I see."

"Yes, but..." Emma looked down, and he noticed her cheeks glowed a shade of dark red. She did not look like a boy as he'd hoped. Rather, the long ducks fell far past her knees and the worn shirt was a little too fitted. She looked like a young girl wearing her brother's shirt and her papa's breeches. The skin of her bare feet looked soft and pearly. He lifted his gaze to find her staring at him with a frown.

"Well," she complained in a churlish voice, "I did the best I could in the pitch dark."

"Yes," he allowed. Phillip eyed her hair knotted in a single long braid down her back. "I suppose you know you don't look like a cabin boy."

"Why can't I wear my gown?" Emma picked it up off the floor from where she'd rolled it up. It was still soaked and oozing water.

"You can bring it along," offered Phillip. "I'll put it with my things." His gaze traveled up her legs from her ankles. Her calves slightly bowed before reaching to her slender thighs.

"Can I get a coat?" she pleaded. She crossed her arms over herself.

"You could, but no," he amended. "Mine would be too big on you. This will just have to do."

She let out a heavy breath. "I feel ridiculous and quite exposed."

Phillip mentally slapped his face and stepped back remembering the plan—or the lack of one. "Well, now, tuck your braid in your shirt. Keep your head down once we go aloft, and I'll fetch you one of Chekilli's old straw hats for you to tug over your face until we paddle away."

"Who?" she sniffed. "Why are we getting off? This is your ship, is it not?"

"It is, and I have two of them," Phillip explained. "The *Mary Alice* and the *Revenge* are not one and the same. The crew aboard the *Mary Alice* does not know you're aboard, and it's best if they don't recognize you, either."

"I guess you're right." Emma rubbed her arms and looked around as if beginning to understand. "I don't wish to put anyone in danger." She hesitated and met Phillip's examination. "Even you."

He put a hand to his heart and chuckled. "Me? I thought you wanted me to be captured and dragged to the gibbets along the Thames?"

She shifted her gaze and gave a quiet laugh. "Well, you did come through after all, although I did not get to tell Roseline goodbye, and she will be devastated." She looked up, and her eyes misted. "She might even think I am dead."

"The deader the better," Phillip told her with a wince. "Perhaps once you reach Charleston you can send her a missive. Something private."

"Yes, perhaps." In a dazed voice, Emma asked, "Phillip, how will I get to Charleston?"

Phillip realized she had not thought any further past being kidnapped than he had smuggling her off the *León*. He grimaced but decided to be truthful. "I haven't planned that far ahead. Let us get you to the bayou and then we will sort it all out."

"The bayou?" she said in surprise. "I thought you sailed the *Revenge*."

"All in good time, Emma," he assured her and reached for her hand, "and you must swear to keep the bayou's secrets."

"I do," she returned without hesitation. "I swear."

Phillip looked into her eyes. "You must keep it, or my honor is stained, and good people will die."

"I swear," she repeated in astonishment, her eyes round and solemn.

A shout sounded from amidships, and Phillip heard the pulleys releasing the lines. The skiff to the river mouth was being prepared, which meant Chekilli had signaled from the distance. "Good. Now, first thing, we must get past the crew of *Mary Alice*."

CHAPTER ELEVEN

Getting past the crew was easy. Emma trailed behind Phillip with her head down like an obedient servant. He stopped at a small cabin and retrieved a frayed hat and plunked it on her head. With a satisfied grunt, he motioned for her to follow him, and she trailed him to the top deck, swaying woozily with the ship as it struggled to find its balance without the wind in her sails.

There were a few murmurs on the wind and then surprised silence when she followed Phillip to the rail. Phillip made a great show of shaking hands and bidding farewell to Captain Page who did not bother to notice her. She scurried into the boat at Phillip's command and found herself seated forward as he climbed in behind her before they were lowered to the water.

She peered across the green-blue waves toward thickly-treed terrain once they were clear of the hull of the ship. There was a river mouth, and she guessed that it was their destination as Phillip picked up an oar and began to stroke toward it. Behind them, the *Mary Alice* caught her wind and continued on her way.

Speaking over her as if she were not there, Phillip mumbled to himself as he paddled into the river and fought the current to move them upstream. The sun beamed down like a hot iron, burning Emma through the thin shirt until she squirmed and fanned herself.

"We're almost there," announced Phillip in a deep voice, and she breathed a sigh of relief as she saw the waterway begin to narrow. Great oaks with branches the size of canoes stretched over the water throwing beams of shade here and there. Old mangrove trees stretched their spidery roots across the shallow bank making underwater caverns for shellfish and seahorses. There was a peaceful quiet broken only by the occasional tern or long-legged heron. It reminded her of the South Carolina low country—and alligators.

"What is this place?" Emma couldn't resist asking. The warning cry of something wild in the trees made a noise that shamed her back into silence.

Phillip answered in a soft voice. "The crew calls it *peligroso* waters, and we are heading into the swamps so keep your eye out for colossal alligators and be on your guard."

Emma sucked in a breath and stiffened. She heard Phillip make a noise in his throat that sounded like a laugh. He was probably teasing her, but she couldn't stop her gaze from roaming over the banks and shallows.

The sunlight mingled with shadows. Emma's palms became damp, and she clutched the hard seat unable to relax until they reached a small, sandy shore. Phillip dragged the boat into the shallows and then helped her out. Her feet splashed down into sucking, unpleasant mud, and she shuddered. Rather than admit her discomfort, Emma squared her shoulders. "It's not much different than home," she insisted. She started in surprise when a dark man with long ebony hair emerged from the trees.

Phillip greeted him in a strange tongue, and Emma locked her jaws together and tried to look confident. The stranger's eyes drifted over her as Phillip and he conversed, and she looked away. Clearly, there were people here Phillip knew and wanted to protect besides the crews on his ships.

Phillip whispered another word or two then raised a hand in goodbye. He glanced back at Emma. "This is Chekilli. He is my right hand on the *Revenge*."

Emma nodded hello like her tongue was tied. The stranger mumbled something to her in the language foreign to her ears then disappeared. "Where'd he go?"

"To fetch the others."

"Oh." Emma looked around instead of asking, "What others?" Did the crew of the *Revenge* hide out in the bayou? She swatted at a buzzing sound near her ear. No wonder they had not been apprehended. She watched Phillip drag the boat further up onto the sand.

"Give me a hand, will you?"

She heaved and tugged until they dragged the boat into some low-lying bushes. Then like a magician, Phillip reached in and pulled out a long and narrow canoe.

"What's that?"

"It's a pirogue, Emma. Now help me get it into the water."

Abashed at Phillip's exasperation, she lugged her end into the water watching for signs of alligators like Mr. McKay had taught her. Seeing nothing, she climbed in, wobbled it, and almost overturned. Phillip seized the sides and snorted. "Confound it, Emma. You'd make a terrible pirate and a clumsy sailor to boot."

"I didn't know this would be a part of the bargain," she sniped, then swatted at another irritating mosquito buzzing as loud as a bumblebee. She was surprised there was yet another leg on the water for their journey. Surely the surroundings would grow worse.

Phillip waded through the brackish water, gave the tiny pirogue a push, and climbed back inside without tossing them both into the drink. The canopy thickened, and Spanish beard dangled longer from the oaks like ghostly lace. "It almost feels like home," she mused. She has seen so little of Florida, she realized, locked away in her hacienda.

Phillip passed an oar and explained how to use it which she did so clumsily, but in truth, she remembered how and found it exhilarating. They could not be that far from Pensacola, yet here she was without the silk cloaked layers expected from Don Marcos. Rather, she was dressed in the comfortable but shocking wardrobe of a young man wearing only her stays underneath and no shoes. Emma licked her lips and concentrated on paddling harder.

"Are you afraid?" Phillip's question broke the quiet around them.

"I'm not. I spent a great deal of time in the low country. Mr. McKay even taught me to fish."

"Impressive."

Emma would have shrugged, but she supposed it was impressive for a don's daughter.

"Perhaps I could hire you on one of my fishing boats."

She chuckled at his teasing. "I wouldn't mind. I can do hard work although you haven't seen me do any."

Phillip fell silent for a few minutes then asked, "You are still determined to go to Charleston then."

"What choice do I have," Emma murmured. "I always hoped to visit one day, but living there again is the only choice I can see." She looked over her shoulder and smiled at him, unable to admit a part of her trusted him enough to follow him to his island home in the Indies and perhaps even stay if she would ever be wanted. Instead, she said, "You could visit me in Charleston. I wouldn't tell your secrets."

He winked at her as she turned back. "I'll keep yours, too," she heard him whisper. His sincerity brought the longing ache to her bones again. Here was someone she could tell anything, and he would listen and not laugh—and keep it to himself.

A haunting silence fell around them. Just when Emma began to wonder how much further they would travel, Phillip guided the pirogue toward a small opening in the trees along a rather unscrupulous-looking embankment that looked to be floating on top of the water. He climbed out in his capable black boots and pulled the pirogue toward the gnarled branches of overturned trees. He helped her out, and she stumbled onto the moist earth with uncertainty.

Phillip tied the little boat off then flung a bag over his back. Motioning for her to follow, he started down a barely discernible footpath, stopped at a tree with an ominous large hollow, and pulled out a sharp silver machete. Wielding it before him like a cutlass, he flicked away vines and briars as they traveled inland across squelchy mud and clusters of tall grass until the earth solidified. The variety of trees and leaves and green needles almost gave the swamp a forest-like feeling but for the jungle of palms and grasses in the murk.

Sweat trickled down her spine, and Emma bit her lip. It was hot. She was thirsty. She shuddered every time her bare feet squelched in the mud or set upon something slimy, but she refused to complain out loud. This was still a world she knew better than Spain.

Pensacola and her chambers in the hacienda seemed far away as the time dragged on. Her shoulders drooped and so did her enthusiasm. What had she done insisting Phillip steal her away without suggesting some kind of plan?

He came to an abrupt stop, and she bumped into the back of him. He did not move but stayed rooted to the spot. Emma pushed back the brim of her hat and peered around him. She felt her jaw drop. In a clearing of trees standing so tall it was surrounded by their upper branches, a cabin towered over them on spindly stilts. A narrow porch wrapped around it. Emma examined the swamp house closely and wondered who lived there. Odds and ends hung from the porch railings like wares. Withered flowers and plants were drying out beneath the roof beams. She stared in fascination. "Is this your hideout?" she queried in the gloom.

"No," snapped an angry voice, "it's mine!"

"QUEENIE OBA!" PHILLIP greeted his mentor-mother-and-divine protector like he'd just returned home for Christmas. She glared at him with such fury he saw flickers of fire in her black eyes. He fought to keep a grin from melting off his lips. "I can explain," he began as if he'd just brought her a puppy, but she didn't move or drop her hands from her generous hips. He stopped at the bottom rung of the ladder and looked up. "There was an unexpected change of plans."

"I'm not blind," Queenie retorted. "I see the Spanish girl."

Feeling Emma tense behind him, Phillip replied, "American actually, although yes, Miss Montego is the don's daughter." He stepped aside and let the two women examine each other like cats. It was clear who the kitten was. Reaching back and taking her hand, Phillip pulled Emma forward.

"Queenie, this is Emma. She fled Pensacola Harbor to avoid being shipped to Spain and married off." He glanced back at Emma whose eyes looked wide and bright as if she'd never seen a powerful or noblewoman before. "Emma," he gently warned, "this is Queenie Oba, and this is her bayou. We are guests here," he added meaningfully.

After another scraping glare across Phillip's face, Queenie stood tall and rigid for several long seconds then with a sharp wave, stepped back and beckoned him up the ladder. He scrambled up and motioned for Emma to follow which she did easily. When she finally clambered up to the porch, he noticed her feet were caked with mud and her legs stained up to her knees. There were dirty streaks smeared across her cheeks and forehead and down her neck.

"She looks like a filthy mongrel," complained Queenie marching into the cabin. "Where are her shoes?" She looked back in disdain. "The don can't provide a pair of boots for his own child?"

Phillip grabbed Emma's hand again and guided her to the open door. "She lost them in the harbor," he explained. Queenie flopped down into her rocking chair and stared. "It's a long story." Phillip stepped inside but just before he pulled Emma over the threshold, Queenie held up her hand and said, "Stop." She pointed at Emma's filthy feet." She can't come in like that and wipe off your boots."

Phillip backed out of the door, and Emma darted out of view of the woman. "Phillip! Where are we? Who is that?"

"Don't worry," he assured her. He looked around for the washing bucket and saw a towel drying on the railing. He snatched it for Emma. "Here." He motioned toward her legs. "Wash off with this."

She took it with a frustrated exhale. "Well, she does not want me here."

"It takes her awhile to trust anyone," he promised her. "This is the safest place for you for now."

Phillip wiped off his boots after Emma finished cleaning up and then rapped on the doorframe. Queenie grunted, and he stepped inside dragging Emma behind him. Her hands were no longer hot and sticky but warm and trembly. He rubbed his thumb across the top of her hand to calm her.

"I wanted you to meet," explained Phillip, and Queenie raised her eyes to the ceiling and let her gaze travel around the room without looking back at him. "I know you're concerned that helping a don's daughter might bring trouble to the bayou, but I could not turn my back on a woman who wants to be free."

Queenie jerked her head back and slit her eyes at him. "Don't you use that excuse with me, Phillip-boy. She's white as a turnip, and her father's a powerful man. She's freer than any woman I know."

Phillip glanced at Emma who looked too frightened and fascinated to speak. He widened his eyes and motioned his head toward Queenie to get her to say something. She was behaving like Don Marcos was in the room, and she felt too intimidated to utter even a word. He squeezed her hand and motioned toward Queenie again.

Emma cleared her throat. "I, uh," she stammered, glancing back and forth between the two, "I am the daughter of Don Marcos," she admitted, "but my mother was from Charleston. I was, I am, I mean, I was born there and came here six years ago," she clarified. "He is sending me to Spain to live with a relative until I find someone of his acquaintance with titles and land to marry."

"Land," spat Queenie as if she understood.

"Yes," agreed Phillip. "She is being traded off like a horse," he said, and Emma squeezed his hand back hard and painfully. Fighting down a chuckle, he continued, "Not a thoroughbred, however," he looked back at her unable to resist giving her a teasing grin. "She is a mongrel, you know, only half of one people and half of another."

"Like many of us." Queenie gave him a dead-eyed stare beneath her silver brows shaped like crescent moons.

Phillip motioned toward Emma. "She boarded the *León* this morning," he admitted, "then snuck off onto the *Mary Alice*. Billy dropped us here.

"Then go get your boat," ordered Queenie.

"I plan to, but I need somewhere safe for her to stay. I can't drag her through the swamp and into the *Revenge's* camp.

Queenie stared. "So you bring her to my house?"

Phillip took an anxious breath. "I had no choice, Queenie. I will pay you handsomely for it."

"Oh," she retorted, "you will."

"May she, can she, stay overnight? She's sworn to keep our secrets." Emma squeezed his hand. He caressed her back, and she stilled.

Queenie began rocking in her chair. There was a cruel moment of silence while Emma trembled, and Phillip held his breath. Finally, Queenie spoke: "I won't turn my Phillip's woman out," she raised a finger and jabbed it at him, "but you fetch her at dawn and get out of my bayou."

Phillip exhaled with relief. "Thank you," he breathed, resisting the urge to cross the space between them and embrace her. "I knew I could count on you."

"*Mmmph*," grunted Queenie. Phillip led Emma over to his favorite low and comfortable horse-hair stool. "You sit right there," he told her in a low tone, and she gave him a wide-eyed, panicked look.

"Is there anything I can do for you now?" Phillip lowered himself to the floor and sat cross-legged near Queenie's feet. "Before I leave, is there anything I can do?"

Queenie's chair made small musical squeaks in time with her swaying motion. She pointed over her shoulder toward the back of the cabin. "You go clean my fish," she commanded but the outside corners of her eyes softened. "I'll cook you and the girl dinner before you go."

"Yes, Queenie," Phillip agreed, hopping to his feet. He gave Emma a fleeting look as he hurried outside. She'd collected herself and sat primly on the stool with legs together and her hands clasped in her lap. Queenie stopped rocking with a jerk and leaned forward.

"Tell me about Charles Town," she demanded, and Phillip heard the soft tones of Emma's reply about Charleston as he closed the door behind him and pulled Queenie's catch of the day out of a cask of cool water.

QUEENIE OBA WAS THE most fascinating woman Emma had ever laid eyes on. She seemed regal and poised; intelligent and wise. Her fingers curled with age, and her forearms were scarred with pink lines and bumpy blotches that had never healed after being severely scraped or burned. But it was Queenie's face that mesmerized Emma the most.

The woman of the swamp had smooth cheeks. They draped around her thick velvet lips the color of the darkest rosebuds. There were pleasant crinkles around her big eyes like an artist had sketched accents around them. The whites were bright and clear, but her pupils were so deep and dark they looked black except for flecks of gold and brass that sparked when she spoke.

Emma meekly answered all of her questions. She explained how her mother died and she was raised with the McKays. She told her how Don Marcos had sent Roseline when she turned seventeen and what was expected of her at the hacienda. When Queenie asked about the courtyard garden, Emma wondered how she knew of it but described the lemon and orange and persimmon trees in great detail. She told her of her spacious room and bed, admitted to the half-dozen silk gowns and the black petticoats she wore to church, and told her how she'd never been allowed to be alone or go anywhere without a chaperone.

Queenie smirked at this, and suspecting she knew, Emma admitted to her midnight walks and wading on the shore. Rather than judging her, Queenie asked about her shells, and

Emma told her they'd been abandoned aboard the *León* which made her sad indeed. Glancing around the cabin, Emma saw conch shells the size of pumpkins and a great many dangling chimes made of shells and coral that she much admired.

Queenie Oba noticed it and relented that they had that much in common. When Phillip returned with the stinking gutted fish, he was ordered back out the door to stoke a fire, and Emma followed her hostess outside and learned how to smoke fish on a buccan and recited the herbs the swamp witch used to season them. They ate on some rather nice china stamped with the East India Trading company mark, and afterward, Queenie returned to her rocker and motioned Emma to the back of the cabin to wash and dry them on her own.

She did so out back, grateful for a few minutes to herself. Her stomach ached from being clenched all day. She hadn't washed a dish in a half-dozen years and found the labor calming and satisfying. Her gown was still soaked, so she wrung it out and hung it over a railing to dry. When she returned and stacked the dishes back onto the shelf as directed, she discovered many fascinating odds and ends in a variety of glass and porcelain jars.

The smooth tones of Phillip and Queenie's conversation died away. When she faced them, Emma saw Phillip sat on the horsehair stool. He met her eyes with something that looked like approval then jumped to his feet.

"I should go." He ran his hands through his hair that gleamed like sunset in the glow of Queenie's lanterns. Emma wanted to beg him to stay. Everything felt strange and unsure. She felt safe with Phillip at her side. She opened her mouth to speak but realized with disquiet Queenie would be witness to anything she had to say. "Thank you," she uttered instead. "I know I've caused you both a great deal of inconvenience, and I promise to be as little trouble as possible until I reach Charleston again."

"Wonderful." Phillip's gaze wandered over her making her aware of her clinging, dirty, cabin boy clothes. "And thank you for protecting me in Pensacola," he added in a frank tone. "It could have been disastrous for us."

Emma gave a shy curtsy certain it looked ridiculous with her attire. She'd done little for him, she knew, other than to keep his secret.

"I must remind you to never speak of this place or Queenie," he insisted, motioning at his peculiar friend.

"I will never breathe a word." Emma heard Queenie grunt in doubt and wondered if she would make her take a blood oath. Phillip picked up his things, crossed the room, and made an awkward bow. "I will see you at dawn."

"Don't you be late," interjected Queenie from behind them.

Phillip raised a brow at Emma like this was a joke then left her alone in the cabin with his mysterious patroness. Emma dropped back onto the stool. She studied her hands waiting for Queenie to ask more questions. Instead, the woman pointed across the room.

"You sleep up there," she declared, and Emma turned to see a frail ladder built into the wall. There was a space of roof missing along the roofline, and she realized she would bed down in a loft for the night—a ceiling space probably cluttered with rats and spiders and bats. She suppressed a shudder. "Yes, madam."

Queenie rocked.

"Now?"

The woman smiled. "You answered well today, and I'm satisfied you're not a spoiled idiot, but you haven't asked me any questions of your own."

"I wasn't sure if they would be welcome."

Queenie's face bloomed into an amused smile that made her look youthful. Her hand went to a long, hideous necklace that looked like it was made out of animal bones and claws, and she began to rock again. "Phillip-boy risked his life for Queenie more than once. He risked his life for you." *Rock.* "You may ask me three questions."

Emma hesitated. Her mind had swirled with questions when she'd first arrived, but none of them seemed to matter now. She felt safe and hidden here, and comfortable, too. Perhaps it was the burning candles caked with flower bits or the gleaming lanterns or maybe even her full belly from some of the best fish she'd ever tasted. "Well..." All she could think of was Phillip. How did he fit in here? The woman watched her like an owl. Emma pressed her lips together and tried to think. Queenie smiled. "How - how did you come to the bayou?"

"I came to Florida from Jamaica," answered the woman. "Phillip and Chekilli built me this place."

"Oh." That was interesting, Emma admitted to herself. Why would Phillip build a home in the middle of a dreadful swamp? She had two left, she knew.

Queenie rocked and stared. "What do you want to know, Emma?" Her tone sounded quite tender as her fingers skirted around the bones on her necklace as if searching for one in particular. Was she Phillip's mother, wondered Emma, but how? He was so very red and white, and she was a woman of nations, of Africa, a continent of kings and queens.

"You want to know about Phillip," Queenie guessed.

Flushing, Emma nodded.

"You've brought great danger to the bayou," she informed Emma in a serious tone, "and to my Phillip-boy."

Emma grimaced. "I didn't mean to."

"He should not have interrupted your shell walk," grumbled Queenie.

Emma shook her head. "I shouldn't have sneaked out all alone."

Queenie's face remained impassive, but she asked, "Why not?"

Emma stared. The answer was obvious, but then again...

"Are you afraid to be alone?"

"No. I've been alone most of my life," Emma admitted, "but it's not in my nature. I don't want to be, and I didn't feel lonely looking for shells and watching the turtles creep up on the shore."

"The shore doesn't belong to anyone," muttered Queenie. "It's God's earth. God made the land, and He can break it up all again and take it back if He wants."

There really wasn't anything wrong with going for a walk, Emma realized. Queenie was right.

"Phillip should not do business in Pensacola and leave his people in the bayou." Queenie rubbed the bones. "His grace is running short and thin."

"I'm concerned about him." Emma squeezed her hands tight. "He says he's a pirate, that he takes things from people who took from him, but I— He kept my secret, even though he was quite ungentleman-like about it in the beginning." Emma recalled Pablo's remarks to Don Marcos about Phillip. "He was seen coming out of the treasury to give a man a loan to recoup his losses aboard one of the merchantmen. They say he pays the widow of his property a greater amount of rent than is necessary. Even Don Marcos says it's too generous." Emma stopped, realizing she was blathering on. "I simply don't understand it."

"Yes, Phillip is too generous," complained Queenie. She rocked a few more times. "He takes from the big boats and shares it with the poor folk," she chuckled. "He keeps two crews, two boats, and he's a big man in Kingston with a fine fat house."

"That's what they say, that he's rich, but I – I know how, and I just don't approve."

"Queenie doesn't approve either, child. Phillip worked hard with his own two hands and my schooling to become a rich man, but he turned to pirating as soon as he was able—after the Redcoats left Pensacola and carried him away."

"They took him to Jamaica?"

"That's where he started."

"And he helped you... escape?"

"I knew Florida before any white man, and you ask too many questions, child. You're all out, but I have another one for you."

"Yes?" Emma stared.

"If they catch my Phillip-boy and try to hang him as a pirate, do you love him enough to sacrifice everything dear and save him as he saved you?"

Emma blinked and looked away. The thought of Phillip being captured made her breathless with fear. And why had Queenie said love *enough*? Did she think Emma was in love? Emma forced her gaze to slide around the room rather than look Queenie in the eye. Of course, Phillip was too bold, too confident, and over-rationalized his reasons for sailing the *Revenge*. It was dreadful, yes, that the actions of a few British soldiers killed his family, but he could never bring back what he loved by carrying on like a cutthroat buccaneer. Why, if he was half the gentleman he pretended to be, she'd love him very much indeed. Even Don Marcos could not deny he was suitable enough for...

For what? What was she thinking? Emma caught herself twisting the don's bracelet still encircling her wrist. *Mi corazón.*

Queenie she saw, was staring with a sly smile on her face. "The sun is setting on Captain Redbird, I fear," she whispered. "He'll need a shooting star to light his way home. Something unexpected. And fearless."

Emma felt her cheeks flood with heat, and her heart warmed, too, as feelings spread throughout her limbs like she'd sipped a drink of warm tea. "Yes," she blurted, without thinking any further, "I would do anything to save Phillip if it was in my power." With a quiet start, Emma realized she truly meant every word.

CHAPTER TWELVE

Phillip flopped like a fish back and forth in the hammock he'd strung between two trees. The camp around him had finally quieted, and he sighed with relief. The crew was anxious for the early start, but no one asked questions about the guest he'd told them would be aboard. She was his prisoner in a way, or under his protection at least, and she would sail with them to Kingston where he would find an American vessel to carry her home if that was the desire of her heart.

It made his chest squeeze painfully to think of her standing alone on the wharves of Charleston. She'd told him herself she had nowhere to go. It hurt his heart to know she'd fallen in love with West Florida and didn't want to leave, but there was no choice.

With a grunt, he flopped over and stared between the palm leaves at the midnight sky. He could easily provide shelter for her in Kingston, he thought. No one knew her there. If she liked it, if she could tolerate their British counterparts and society, maybe she would stay. He liked that idea. Loved it. With the don and Captain Gonzalez out of the way, maybe there could be something more than a deal between them. The idea made him almost breathless. He thought sleep would never come.

At sunrise, the irritating gulls and their arguing roused Phillip before the sun broke fully over the horizon. He jumped out of his hammock and rolled his things into it before striding to the small but deep bay where the *Revenge* floated on the tide. It was already beginning to stream away as the moon drifted out of sight, and he rushed aboard to check the supplies and wash up and change.

Revenge was a sleek vessel made of Jamaican redwood with two masts and a flush deck. Light cannons lined the two uppers—not too many but enough to pepper a hull or mizzenmast. These days just a black flag did the job. She'd been a coastal gunship before he purchased her stolen in Tobago. He'd given her a fresh overhaul with the best lines and sheets and plenty of ammunition.

The crew came aboard in groups like curious ants but soon set to rights storing their ditty boxes and turning to their duties. Phillip threw back a cup of coffee, righted his clean white shirt, and brushed back his hair. He clipped a long string of red feathers into it, tied the matching scarlet sash around his waist, and set his cocked hat on his head at his favorite angle. He'd shaved, finding beards and scruff uncomfortable and unseemly for a gentleman pirate.

The bosun shouted, and he rushed out of the cabin, slowing his steps when he saw Chekilli come aboard with Emma close behind him. She did not look pleased with her escort although they were familiar, and when her eyes met his, her mouth settled into a straight, unhappy line after dropping open in surprise at his appearance.

He strode across the deck to greet her. "Miss Montego," he declared. She looked rather pretty and ordinary in her dried gown. It was simple compared to her wardrobe in Pensacola, but still fine. Without heavy layers of petticoats, it draped around her waist and trailed to the tops of her—He stared.

"I lost my shoes," she reminded him in a churlish tone as if she hadn't slept well. "Your friend gave me these to wear."

He gave her an amused stare then motioned for her to follow him. They dropped down a hatch. Her room would be the small storage closet below his cabin—suitable for a pair of ships' boys to share. He pushed open the door. "These are your quarters. I'm sure it isn't anything like your chambers in the hacienda, but it is spacious even for the *Revenge*."

"Thank you," she approved in a crisp tone. She brushed past him and dropped a small hemp sack Queenie must have loaned her onto the simple cot with its thin blanket.

"I'm afraid since you left your things aboard the *Mary Alice* you will have to make do with a few borrowed items." He tried to grin, but his teasing did not affect her.

"I'm sure I'll survive."

He cocked his head at her. "Are you angry with me after I kept my end of the deal? Did you not enjoy your night in the swamp?"

"With the spiders and bats?" she shot back. Emma plopped onto the edge of the cot. Her hair was woven into a single braid down her back. Gone were the curls and pins. The style accentuated her strong cheekbones and the curve of her jaw. "I didn't expect you would leave me alone there and with a woman who had not expected any guests."

"You seemed to get on well enough."

"Yes, we did after all, but I didn't know where you'd gone off to or if you'd be back. Then Mr. Chekilli arrived this morning in your place."

"Yes, well," excused Phillip while he gazed up at a beam for emphasis, "I did have a ship to ready and a course to plot."

Emma lowered her glaring eyes to the boards at her feet. "Then I'll thank you for sending for me. I am anxious to be off is all, before the guards come searching, and I certainly did not want to be found in Queenie's bayou and cause her any trouble."

"There is nothing but smooth sailing ahead," Phillip promised her, "but I must ask you to keep to your quarters here. My crew is a superstitious lot and will blame every unfortunate event on your presence."

"That's ridiculous. I've never brought anyone bad luck. Of course I will stay as you ask." Suddenly Emma glanced at him through her dark, long lashes. "As anxious as I am about what comes next, a great burden has been lifted from my heart. I'm overcome with relief I'm not on my way to Havana, Phillip." He saw her eyes glisten. "Of course I'm riddled with guilt that Roseline knows nothing of my safety, but I do hope she knows me well enough to believe I am quite capable of taking care of myself."

"Of course you are," agreed Phillip. "Any woman that can march through a swamp in her bare feet without complaint is a woman to be taken seriously."

She pursed her lips at his teasing tone. "I'm sure these thick hide boots will serve me well, and they're quite comfortable."

He glanced down again at the Creek moccasins with approval. They fit like short boots and protected her ankles from the mud. With tiny glass beads embroidered into the shapes of flower petals, they looked much like ones he'd seen Queenie wear. It made his mind spin with affection for the stern woman he cherished as a mother. It was a valuable pair.

Orders given overhead rumbled through the beams. "See now, I am off to pirate, Señorita, so do keep to your quarters, please. We have no seashells hidden aboard that need collecting."

Emma sniffed at him and smiled at the same time. "You won't even know I'm here," she promised. He gave a slight bow and backed out of the cabin to allow her to shut herself in. *Well, Miss Montego*, he thought, *there is nothing you can do to make me forget it.*

IT SEEMED TO TAKE FOREVER before the *Revenge* began to move outside Emma's diminutive porthole. She was certain it was too small for a cannon barrel. She watched the shallow brown water of the inlet deepen to blue as the ship jerked past giant oaks and towering pine trees on the shore. Just as the muggy air sulking in her little closet seemed to lighten, a fresh gust blew inside, and she stood again to watch the sandy coast drop away. Light shallows stretched for as far as she could see. She heard the eager wind snapping through the lines and the flap and pop of the sails as they caught the breeze. Soon, the *Revenge*, the sleek fabled schooner she had heard so much about, increased her pace, and Emma relaxed with relief that she was on her way.

It was almost funny, she thought to herself, that she felt so calm aboard an actual pirate ship. Maybe it was because of the captain. Phillip looked quite different in his dark boots and light breeches. An exotic woven sash knotted around his waist made him look trim below his wide shoulders—and dangerous. With a cocked hat and an odd collection of red feathers trailing down his back, he looked like a legend's hero—or villain.

Amused, Emma settled back onto the cot and closed her eyes. She listened to the murmurs of the crew and their feet padding across the planks overhead until a sharp knock roused her, and she realized she'd fallen asleep. She sat up and smoothed her hair then clambered up to open the door. A young man with sallow skin and curious light green eyes stared for three counts then gave a clumsy bow. "The captain wishes to speak with you."

Emma glanced past him through the narrow passage. "Where?" The boy pointed up, and she nodded. Reaching for the straw hat Queenie had generously loaned her, Emma followed the boy who could not be that many years younger than she up a steep ladder to the top deck.

Phillip towered over the other men mingling around the ship's wheel. She wound her way around the lines and past suspicious gazes. He held out an arm, and she slipped hers through. They walked the deck until there was a space free of clutter and bodies.

"I thought you would like some fresh air and to stretch your legs before we dine."

"I thank you."

"How are your sea legs coming along?"

"I'm sure I don't have them yet," Emma replied. She gazed over the stunning view of endless water that stretched like a blue desert to the bottom of the heavens. The wind skipped across the back of her neck in a pleasant caress. "I'd never been to sea until Don Marcos sent for me," she revealed, "and I didn't find it intolerable." She glanced at Phillip and his strong profile studying the distant horizon beside her. He was quite handsome even with the strange hat and feathers. She would miss him very much when they parted, she thought with a tug at her heart.

"Do you think you will send word to your father at some point?" wondered Phillip.

"Don Marcos? I'm not certain. I think perhaps it's best this way."

"Do you?" He looked at her oddly. "Then I suspect he will go to his grave with regrets."

Emma peered at him. "What do you mean? I am out of his life either way."

He cocked his head. "I thought he felt rather fond of you."

She gave a sharp shake of her head, "I'm sure he is not. He hardly spoke to me except to coordinate our schedules."

"He wanted you to be settled and happy before he passed, I suspect." Emma pursed her lips in disagreement. "He is ill, yes. Roseline says he doesn't have long to live."

"So he did love you."

Emma wrinkled her brow and found Phillip's searching eyes tainted with surprise.

"He kept you at his side at events and parties, and rode with you around town in that ridiculously ornate carriage."

"Yes, and I was an ornament, too," Emma pointed out.

"Oh, I don't know," Phillip mused. "The don threw you parties and boasted of your accomplishments at meetings and dinners." He glanced down at her wrist. "He gave you that lovely bracelet, and he didn't own that carriage until you arrived."

"And you remember that?"

"Of course, I do. It's a small settlement. Your presence did not go unnoticed whenever I was in port."

Hmm, thought Emma, curious that he should have noticed her long before she did him. He elbowed her. "Are you saying you don't remember me or the *Mary Alice* in the harbor before you started sneaking out for seashells?"

Emma angled her chin to let the breeze brush over her cheeks. The way Phillip spoke, it was as if Don Marcos loved her like a real daughter instead of thinking her a burden. "I knew there was an American," she admitted, "but I did not pay much attention to anyone."

"You were as much a foreigner as I," he relented, "but your Spanish is very well, and you look the part."

"What do you mean?" She looked over to find him staring. "Well," he answered in a throaty tone, "you clearly have your father's eyes and are close to his complexion, so I can only deduce you have your mother's features and beauty."

Staring directly into one another's eyes so closely and with Phillip's more intimate tone, Emma felt her cheeks blaze. She clutched the rail to keep from looking weak-kneed at his words. Beside her, Phillip's tanned and lined hand brushed against hers. She glanced sideways at him and found him studying her again.

"You are the kindest and most humble girl, Emma," he declared. He cleared his throat and looked away. "And very intelligent and brave."

Emma felt a rush of tingly heat pour down her neck and drip to her toes. She only felt such fires when she was with Phillip. No one had ever said such lovely things, and they were things she tried so hard to be.

"Thank you, Phillip," she stammered. Her breath seized in her ribcage, and she wondered if he knew he'd won her over, how he made her feel safe and gave her courage at the same time. "There are so few people in the world I find I can trust," she admitted and forced a shy chuckle. She glanced around the ship at the rather normal and harmless looking men. "Which is why I don't understand this."

She took a deep breath and made herself face him. "You are good-hearted and fair, open-minded, and fearless. I know you think you're acting in the service of others, Phillip," she rushed on, "but it's wrong, it's against the law."

Emma paused as his mouth turned down in disappointment. "There are ways to help others as Queenie did for you when you were just a boy—other ways than this." She searched his face until he met her eyes. "If you are clever enough to go from a farm boy to a merchant, and a successful one at that, then you are clever enough to find a way to right the world without doing so as a pirate. Really, Phillip," she forced a dry chuckle, "there is so much good around us when we stop looking over our shoulders at the pain in the past." She saw she had his complete attention. "There will never be enough revenge in the world to heal your broken heart, but a little love can do wonders."

Phillip's hard stare softened. Emma felt herself blush and looked away without another pleading word. Oh, how she ached to jump up on her toes and throw her arms around his neck. She wanted to hear his heart beating through his shirt and into her head. She wanted to feel his hands cup her neck and hold her tight. Was this love? Would she ever know it again?

With a tight swallow, Emma squared her shoulders. "Do you think Don Marcos loved me, Phillip?" she inquired in a changed tone. She needed something, anything, to change the mood between them. She'd as good as exposed her heart, something she'd never been able to do for Don Marcos.

He glanced at her then leaned over the rail as if pondering the weather. "My father loved me. I don't see yours behaving any differently." His words made Emma's heart glad in a way she'd never felt before. "And besides," Phillip added, "who could not, Emma?"

PHILLIP DINED IN HIS quarters with his first officers, a common routine, except Emma was invited along which seemed to disquiet the lot of them. She kept her gaze lowered to her plate and did not speak until Chekilli asked her about the Carolina low country. She surprised them all by insisting there were alligators there, along with wildcats and bears.

Phillip defended her pronouncements, having grown up not too far south of her coastal home. "It's just flatter in Florida," he agreed, "and hotter and sandier." Then he shared a memory of boar hunting with his father and older brothers when he was chased and nearly gutted by a wild pig.

After a pleasant plate of sharp sliced cheese and sour persimmons, Emma stood to excuse herself, and he insisted that he join her. Her scalding words from earlier still burned. He left his relieved mates to a round of rum and escorted her back onto the deck.

"Should I go below?" she asked.

It was warm but the breeze licking over the ship felt pleasant. "I'd be happy to take a turn with you before I take the con," offered Phillip as he peered aft at his navigator guiding the ship. He said a silent prayer they would not come upon an unsuspecting merchant from any country, as he did not want Emma to see him or his pirate crew in action. They might have made every endeavor to appear fair and harmless, but they were a threatening lot whose moods could change with just a shift of the wind.

Emma glanced back toward the stern, too. "The coast is out of sight now," she observed.

"Yes, it will only take a few days before we reach Kingston if the weather cooperates." Phillip walked her to the rail and put his back to it. He gazed up the ratlines. "You would find an amazing view up there," he teased. He could just picture himself tossing her over his shoulder and climbing the mast to its highest peak. Would she be frightened of the long swishing and swaying from up above?

Emma looked aloft with interest. "I always wondered what it looked like from up there."

He grinned. "Maybe before this voyage is through, I will carry you to the top." He watched the spotter, Mr. Dabit, lean forward and shade his eyes with his hand. Phillip followed his gaze across the sea. The boson saw him and did the same.

Phillip squinted. There was a crumb on the horizon, a triangular dark shadow almost glowing from the receding sun. He sucked in a breath. Company. Or prey. He'd have to put

Emma down below sooner than he'd hoped. He reached for her hand, and she clutched it. The feeling of her small warm fingers shot a musket ball of desire through him, but it was a need to protect her from the Pirate Redbird and his crew.

Phillip resisted the urge to slap himself upside the head. What had he been thinking? Queenie was right. Filch a nobleman's daughter and sail her to the Caribbean on a pirate ship? Yes, it all felt cozy in the bayou yesterday, almost as if they were a pair. A couple. Together. Today aboard the *Revenge* felt as normal as any other day he'd spent with her, but reality was just over the stern. He might have only been a minor irritation to most in Florida's waters, but he was still a wanted man—or Redbird was.

Chekilli strode across the deck to meet him. His round eyes looked enormous with concern. "Who's that?" he questioned in his direct way.

Sensing Emma's concern at his elbow, Phillip exhaled and took another long look. "I'm not sure. Why they've decided to follow in our wake I would like to know." Tempted, he glanced up the mast again and saw Dabit pitched forward with an eyeglass stuck to his eye.

Phillip ripped off his silly hat, tossed it to the deck, and leaped up the mast climbing as fast as his arms and legs could pull him. He maneuvered around his spotter until they stood shoulder to shoulder. "What's she look like?"

"Spanish," grunted Dabit.

"Spanish?" repeated Phillip in concern. One never knew in these waters. Dabit dropped the eyeglass. "*Guardacosta* it looks like, but she's a generous size and looks heavy.

Phillip held his palm out for the eyeglass and pressed it against his eye. It *was* large for a coastal ship but small for a ship of the line. He studied the configuration of sails and squinted to make out her colorful pennants. "Dash it all," he hissed. "It's the *León*."

"That's what I feared," admitted the spotter, "but I wanted to be sure."

"And I've just left Pensacola," Phillip complained. He looked down and saw the upturned faces of Chekilli and Emma at the foot of the mast. "Sound the alarm," he ordered and began his hurried descent.

Dabit bellowed, and the deck erupted into activity. As soon as Phillip's boots clapped to the deck, Chekilli said, "Well?"

"Guardacosta," acknowledged Phillip. Their eyes met, and Phillip saw the frustration and dread in his friend's eyes.

Chekilli glanced at Emma then back to Phillip. "And what is your plan, amigo?" Phillip swallowed.

"Guardacosta?" Emma questioned in a concerned tone. She studied the growing ship over the stern. "Is it... Is that?"

She couldn't finish, and Phillip wouldn't let her. "You should go below," he commanded, unable to avoid sounding grim. It was his worst nightmare. The absolute worst thing that could happen. He'd promised Chekilli they would not be caught and that no one would be in danger.

"Go on now," he prodded, and Emma stumbled forward toward the hatch, casting one last look of panic over her shoulder.

"She cannot be found aboard," Chekilli insisted. His face looked drawn, serious. He was a generous man, but he drew a hard line when it came to his own survival.

"Yes, I know." Phillip's shoulders felt like heavy cannon-balls. He could barely stand. "We can put her in a cask and hide her in the hold."

"We're on a pirate ship, Phillip. We can't be captured. We won't be."

Phillip took a heavy breath to calm himself. "We've been in worse situations than this, Chekilli. Pull the sails back as tight as they'll go even if the masts complain. We're faster and just have to outrun them until twilight."

"There is nowhere to hide. We'll never reach a cay before nightfall," warned Chekilli.

"We don't need a cay," Phillip insisted, "we just need the wind."

Chekilli grunted loudly in disagreement and turned back to the view over their stern. The *León* had grown in size on the horizon. "She had a head start before we saw her, and she has the wind."

Phillip locked his jaws together. He watched the colors of the distant Spanish flag become distinct. "I've never seen her move like that. She's come out hunting and ready to race."

Chekilli nodded in agreement. "She must have returned to Pensacola or becalmed at Santa Rosa."

"And lightened her load."

"Tossed off half her guns," Chekilli agreed. "She had two dozen but even half that is enough to catch us."

"And enough to fight us," said Phillip in a whisper. It felt like the blood in his body had pooled into his head making it impossible to think. The crew stared quietly after realigning the stays and dropping all sails to flee. The current swished along the sides of the ship in warning, but there was no way to make

Revenge go faster. He was used to being the chaser, not the chased.

Emma's shining crown suddenly popped up through the hatch from where she'd disappeared. Phillip grit his teeth. The last thing he needed was the very person Gonzalez was looking for traipsing around the deck within view. He strode across the vibrating boards as she climbed out.

"What are you doing? I told you to stay below." It was difficult not to sound harsh, but his plans, his life, and his future were slipping through his fingers. Even his great wealth and holdings in the Indies could not save him now. Nothing could.

She walked past him. "Is it the *León*?"

"It is. Now return to your quarters."

"And what?" Emma's forehead lowered over her dark eyes. "They are looking for me, aren't they?"

"Emma," warned Phillip, "you cannot be found. They will hang us all and no excuse will do."

"I know that," declared Emma. She faced him with her fierce eyes, yet she still looked diminutive. "This is my fault."

"Please—"

"No," she shot back. "I forgave you when you backed out of the deal. I felt angry and cheated, but I would have done the same thing in your shoes. Then you came back." She gazed at him with shining eyes. "You came back for me and risked everything, so you... Phillip, forgive me for being selfish and asking you to do this at the risk of others' lives. You've sacrificed everything."

Phillip's throat tightened. As usual, her timing was terrible. She lurked around the settlement's footpaths in the dark of night on his schedule and now she wanted to play the lovely saint at the worst moment of his life. As if reading his mind, Emma stood up on her toes, kissed him firmly in the hollow of his cheek, and shoved her moccasins into his hands. "Here," she whispered, "you give these back to Queenie." She held out the bracelet and pushed it into his hand. "*Mi corazón*," she whispered.

"What are you doing?" Phillip stammered.

Emma looked past him, and he followed her gaze to the horizon in time to see a puff of smoke from the *León's* bow. "Captain Gonzalez would jump overboard for a cat," she murmured.

"What?"

A whizzing cannonball sailed through the distance between them and landed with an ominous splash close to starboard. Emma gasped, and Phillip reached out to steady her and shout if need be, that she must get below and hide.

Phillip squeezed her beloved bracelet in his grip. "Emma..."

Ignoring him, she lifted her skirt and took off at a run across the deck to jump onto the taffrail like a doe. She stopped and grabbed a line, wavered to catch her balance, and then with the grace of a cormorant, leaped off the stern into the air and disappeared into the ocean below.

Phillip stood frozen as if in a dream. His mother's face, his father's face, and his brothers all flashed before his eyes. They'd disappeared. And just like his family, she'd disappeared, too.

He heard Chekilli's commanding voice echo from somewhere far away. The *Revenge* veered to port and continued plowing through the waters like the hounds of hell were behind it, leaving little Emma behind.

Phillip raced to the stern and looked. The *León's* chasers had quieted. No more cannonballs. He scanned the ocean, heart jerking at his soul until tears seeped into his eyes. After what seemed like an eternity, a bobbing little Emma Montego reappeared on the swaying surface waving her arms in desperation for the *León* to halt and rescue her.

She'd kept her part of the deal.

CHAPTER THIRTEEN

Emma opened her eyes with a start. Her lovely room with the wide shutters and long window sill appeared out of nowhere. She sat up with a jerk, and light linens pooled in her lap. It hadn't been a dream after all. Roseline had changed her into a familiar soft chemise, brushed out her tangled, ratty hair, and urged her to drink a sweet, floral tea before tucking her into bed. Without asking, she seemed to know that Emma had been safe all along. Once she murmured, "Who?" and Emma whispered, "A gentleman," and gave her a pleading stare to keep the secret.

She searched the room but did not see her traveling gown. Her bracelet. It was not on the vanity. If it had all been a dream it would be there, sitting on its little velvet bed in its box, but no. It was in Phillip's hands. The pirate Redbird.

Her throat pinched, and she gathered the blanket in her fists. The sound of soft breathing made her turn her head. Don Marcos was reclined in the chair beside her. Roseline had been there when Emma had drifted off to sleep the night before, but now it was her father.

"*Buenos días*," she murmured, examining his pale skin that had taken a yellow turn in only a matter of a week since she had seen him last.

"You slept well, I hope," he answered in a soft tone. He looked like a different man. Had watching her go been more difficult for him than she suspected?

"I did... Papa," she added tentatively. His grave stare softened. "I'm sorry I frightened you and Roseline. I came to no harm, I assure you." She looked down at the blanket clutched in her hands.

"Captain Gonzalez," began Don Marcos, surprising her by switching to English, "says you were kidnapped while aboard the *León* in the harbor and hidden away until you were transferred onto the *Revenge*.

"Yes, it's true."

"You don't know the man or the boat?" he pressed.

Emma shook her head, but she couldn't lie out loud. "What kind of man does that? A desperate man, I suppose, and what does it matter?"

"Well," mused Don Marcos, "a great deal to a great many. I would have paid whatever ransom they asked. Every vessel in the area was hunted down and searched. Roseline felt certain you had run away, but I thought you had fallen overboard and drowned."

He sounded so sad Emma made herself look again. Roseline had whispered in her ear that she knew she'd escaped. She'd even mouthed, "Oakley?" Emma had gripped her friend and companion tightly in reply, but she could not share her secrets.

"I must confess I have been distraught and missed you violently."

She blinked. Don Marcos. Miss her?

As if hearing her question, he said, "I have hardly been out of my bed."

"I know that you are ill, Papa."

He did not bristle at her new form of address. Instead, he smiled at her in a way she'd never seen before. "Yes, daughter, and I have been ill for some time. You would be happier in Spain than to wallow here and watch an old man die."

"But I want to be here," cried Emma, "even if you must leave me." She slid to the edge of the bed, her bare feet brushing the floor. "You are my family, all that I have and all that I need, and Pensacola is my home. I don't want to go away." Her eyes flooded with tears. "I know I was unhappy at first because I did not understand it—this land, the language and customs, and... you." Emma's heart twisted. "I don't have my bracelet anymore," she confessed, "but it meant the world to me that you would give me such a thing."

Don Marcos shifted in his chair. Wrapped in a gold and red silk banyan, he crossed one slippered ankle over another. "I am happy you treasured it so. I have for years. It was a gift for your mother, you see."

"My mama?"

"Sí. I loved her very much, Emma. We came from two different worlds, but her beauty and heart spellbound me the first time I saw her. She was the kindest creature."

"How long before... she died?"

"We did not know each other a year before you came, and she departed. I was not welcome in Charleston, not truly. My wealth was, but there was great disapproval in the colony because she was—"

"Common?"

"Yes. A servant and poor."

"Oh." It all made sense now. Nothing came as a shock to Emma. Of course, her mama would have been a servant. The McKays had been kind and godly, but they had treated her as such.

"Is that why you left me there?"

"With the Catholics?"

"Yes."

"You were an infant, and I could not care for you. Then I had a new assignment to serve in Pensacola, so I came here to heal my heart and forget about her—and you. For that, I am sorry."

Emma looked over at him. "I forgive you. It's easy to do. I was not treated unkindly or spoiled, and it was a happy life in the low country even if it was difficult at times."

"Your brother in Spain has little to do with me, you understand," explained Don Marcos, "because my marriage to his mother was arranged. He had no desire to join me overseas when he was a young man."

"Was he angry when she died?"

"I don't think so, no, but he was unhappy when I wed an American no matter how brief the union. Harsh words passed between us. He has refused to ever set foot in New Spain, and I am too old and sick now to go home."

His hand reached out, and Emma stretched for it. "I'm sorry that he will not come, but it's all well and good, for I don't wish to go. This is my home now, and I am determined to stay. I insist, Papa, that I stay—with you."

He squeezed her hand. "And when I am gone?"

Emma looked away before her eyes watered. She gave a low chuckle. "I will have Roseline, and this lovely home," she hoped.

"Perhaps Captain Gonzalez?"

"Oh, no," she breathed. "I could not. I know he became irritated when I offered so little about Redbird and the *Revenge* after he rescued me, but even so, I cannot settle for less than love like my mama was so brave enough to do."

"Does he know?"

Emma flushed. "I informed him I intended to return to live in Pensacola with you and nowhere else."

"You may have whatever your modest heart desires, *mi corazón*."

Emma finally allowed tears of relief to escape. She took a deep breath. "Thank you, Papa, and no, I will not have everything my heart desires, but it must be enough." He looked at her in question, but she sealed her lips. She wondered where Phillip had sailed away to. Poor Queenie. Because of Emma, he could never come back.

THE HEAT OF LATE JULY only intensified the following month and thereafter. It was too hot to go out, and Emma dared not creep away during the night should Don Marcos need her. Besides, it was too painful to think of hunting seashells in the moonlight when she knew she would never see Phillip again.

Captain Gonzalez called and regretfully informed her he would return to St. Augustine after sailing Roseline to Havana to visit family. When he hesitated with meaning and hope in his eyes, Emma rose to her feet like she had seen Don Marcos do upon dismissing someone. She reminded him her father was ill and that it was best. Despite whatever suspicions he carried over how Emma had come to be aboard the *Revenge*, his disappointment and her confidence finally pushed them all aside. She wished him well, and he departed with a soft frown.

No word came from Kingston. No *Mary Alice* came into port. The rumors the *Revenge* crew had escaped the *León* by throwing their prisoner overboard like savages began to fade as the ship had apparently left the gulf in search of waters with easier pray.

Emma kept to the hacienda. Within weeks, the roles of parent and child were exchanged. Don Marcos grew paler and more sallow. The whites of his eyes turned yellow. He sat for long periods in the shade of the courtyard while Emma hurried back and forth to the house to fetch him anything that would keep him comfortable. By October, he took to bed, and she welcomed the cool of the house even though she sat for hours at his bedside.

While he slept, she wrote letters to Mrs. McKay. When he was awake, she read to him in his native tongue from *Don Quixote* and the Bible. He told her about her mother and what he knew of her family in Dublin. When it was late, and his mind grew wistful, he'd speak of his childhood home in Cuenca and his father and the orchards. Emma told him about the McKay's children, and they talked of the neatly cobbled streets of Charleston. She assured him they were not as magical to her as Pensacola's fairytale beaches and their little hacienda.

One week before Roseline was to return, the sun seemed to want to slip away a little earlier than usual. Emma went to the small stable and requested they bring the carriage around. The don was able to sit up this afternoon and wanted to ride down to the shore. She thought it a good idea and told him she would gather up the brightest shells she could find and bring them to him. He was learning the names of seashells and had sent off for a copy of a botany book they could peruse together, but Emma knew it would not arrive in time.

The groom and driver set off with them toward the harbor where they veered along the seawall and rode out to the sandy shoreline. Papa sent them off to relax once they settled him onto the sand in his sedan with a cushioned chair for Emma. She plopped down for a few minutes and laughed with the don at a pelican stalking a crane for its catch.

"Greedy little pirate," came a voice from behind them. Emma spun in her seat as Papa looked over his shoulder.

Phillip Oakley leaned against a thick water oak just a few paces away. Emma rose to her feet in a slow motion. His hair was clipped quite short in a rather becoming way, and he wore a thick and proper cravat nestled in the crook of his shining blue waistcoat.

"Phillip," she murmured.

"Oh," croaked Don Marcos, "Señor Oakley."

Phillip strolled over and cast Emma a long, intimate gaze that made her tingle from head to foot then he turned to the don. "Don Marcos," he bowed. "I am sorry to find you ill."

"You have returned to Pensacola," observed the don, "but see, I have no business for you at this time." He gave a dry chuckle. "I daresay you will have to find someone else to purchase your sugar and rum, for I will not be around much longer to enjoy it, and Emma, my daughter, prefers her lemon water."

Emma's mind swirled with precautions. Was Phillip here as Captain Redbird or as a merchant? Were the *Revenge* and Chekilli nearby? She pushed her fingernails into her palms.

First and foremost, she had to protect Papa, and then maybe after he was gone...

Phillip bowed to her, too. "You are looking well, Señorita Montego," he greeted her. He stared at her another enduring moment, but she could not tear her eyes away.

"You were going to walk?" Papa reminded her in an amused tone.

She turned to him. "Are you comfortable here?"

"Of course, yes." His gaze danced back and forth between her and Phillip. "You promised me a seashell, daughter."

"Yes, I did," smiled Emma.

Phillip stepped forward. "You don't mind, Don Marcos, if I accompany your daughter down the beach, I hope."

Don Marcos gave his approval with a grave nod. Phillip pretended it was nothing at all and proffered his arm. Gazing up at him, Emma took it then returned her attention to her papa. He was watching her with his head inclined. She had asked about the *Mary Alice* several times over the past few weeks. Was he putting it together? Did he see her surprise and pleasure when she realized who stood behind them?

Phillip escorted her down the beach. She hoped he could not hear her heart thumping. "He does look poorly, I am sorry to say, but you, Miss Montego, do not."

Emma kept her eyes to the sand. "What are you doing here, Phillip? Why have you come?"

"Don't you mean Redbird?"

She tripped, and he steadied her. A familiar bracelet encircled his wrist. "No, I do not. That is not the real you."

"You're right," he agreed with another lazy step. "It is not. In fact, it could not be. There is no Captain Redbird anymore, and the *Revenge* is long gone."

Emma looked at him in surprise. The sun hovered over the water of the bay like a brass orb. It made his hair gleam like copper.

"Come along," he urged with a gentle smile, "we cannot stop and stand so close together with your papa watching."

Emma took a nervous breath and continued walking. "What happened?"

"Forgiveness."

She stopped in frustration. "To the *Revenge,* I meant. The crew. Chekilli. And Queenie Oba!"

"Oh," Phillip waved her off with his free hand. "The *Revenge* has been refitted and renamed and has a new captain."

"You're not—"

He shook his head. Relief streamed through her. "Chekilli?" she guessed.

"That was the deal. I gave it up, and he took over. It's legal as far as I know, and I don't wish to know anything more."

"And Queenie?"

Phillip motioned toward the east. "Queenie is right where you left her, so don't worry. I daresay she won't be happy to see me when I call on her soon, but I did bring a cask of rice from the States if she will have it."

Emma took a deep breath to calm her racing heart. Her stays felt too tight. She gazed up into Phillip's eyes as happiness flooded through her like the streaming tide. "You are no longer a buccaneer?"

"No." He gazed steadily into her as if searching her soul. "I made peace with the past, and I've forgiven the— Well, not every Englishman I meet is responsible for what happened to my family. Or Spaniard," he amended.

"You've given all that up?"

"There comes a time when you have to let go so you can go on," Phillip mused. "A wise woman once told me there will never be enough revenge in the world to heal a broken heart, and a little love can do wonders."

Emma felt herself smile. The hope and his change of heart made her want to kiss him again just as she had before she jumped off his pirate ship. Would he ever feel for her the way she did him?

Phillip shook himself from her eyes, glanced back toward the distant don, then reached down to the ground and picked up a scalloped shell.

"Look at this one, Emma. It's as orange as a melon on one side and as pink as your cheeks on the other." She chuckled and accepted the prize. "I suppose Don Marcos will like it well enough," she approved.

"But then you will have nothing," he teased.

She gazed up at him. "How long will you stay in Pensacola?"

He pressed his lips together for a long pause. The *woosh* and *shhh* of the gentle waves on the shore whispered around them. "I suppose I will stay as long as you will have me," he replied. "I'm a bit of a broken shell myself, you know."

His sincere and hopeful tone lit Emma's heart on fire. She felt herself rise up to her toes but caught herself. "I would like you to stay," she admitted, her eyes brimming, "for as long as possible. Even forever if you wish."

He bowed his head over hers. "Oh, I wish it," he murmured.

"You do?"

"I do." He raised her trembling hand to his lips and kissed it.

"I do, too," she whispered.

He surprised her by dropping to the sand on one knee. Looking up, he dropped her hand and slid off the bracelet and held it out. "Would you make another deal with me, *mi corazón*? Marry me, and I will move my legal and very lucrative business to Pensacola and give up a buccaneer's life."

"For good?"

"Forever."

Emma swallowed back tears and pulled the silly pirate up to his feet. "Of course I will," she laughed. "Sí, Captain Redbird. I wish only to find happiness like my mother and papa, and I know I will have it with you."

Phillip stood with a grin and held out his arms, and Emma leaped into them, throwing herself around his neck and squeezing him tightly so he could never escape.

EPILOGUE

There was a flurry of activity in the upper windows of the hacienda. Phillip Oakley looked up hopefully, but after waiting several moments for the dark cheeks of Roseline to peer out over the wide sill, he gave up and went back to pacing the courtyard.

The orange trees were budding, and he stopped beneath one to examine its branches for any sign of damage or decay. Don Marcos had left him books and a great deal of ledgers listing the seasons and processes required to keep his orchard producing. Like the summer heat, he had faded away in the early winter, a year ago this month past. His daughter had been inconsolable for a great many weeks until she had learned of other family news.

Phillip reached up and plucked a green leaf and smelled it. Soon, all of the trees in Pensacola would be revived as spring came early to these shores. Life, he'd learned, came and went at its own time and there was no use in grieving or dreading it. Whatever went out came back again, much like the tide. Soon, there would be another Montego in New Spain. The don would have a grandchild.

"You are not celebrating yet."

Phillip looked up at the high courtyard wall he'd built between the street and gardens. Billy sat casually on the top of it with one leg bent under his elbow and the other dangling down. "Is there no one to answer the door?"

His friend jumped down with ease and landed on his feet. "I didn't feel much like knocking," he admitted. "Can't a man jump a garden wall every now and then or must we always behave like gentlemen?"

Phillip glanced up at the window again. The gut-wrenching cries of his wife had quieted for what seemed like hours ago. He rubbed his hands together and wheezed in a worried breath. "Sometimes we must." He motioned toward a small table and set of iron chairs. "Come, tell me, how is business?"

Billy looked toward the house and then with a grimace joined him at the table. He plopped down as if unconcerned about Mrs. Oakley. "The *Mary Alice* lost some canvas in the storm last week. I thought I'd drop in and see the owner about repairs."

"I am glad to see you." Phillip lowered his voice. "And how fare our other brothers in the Windwards? Have you heard?"

"Chekilli is a fine coffee bean merchant," answered Billy. He cleared his throat and looked around the courtyard. "—when he is not smuggling out runaways and dropping them off in the bayous along the coast."

"I miss him," Phillip admitted. "He was not there the last time I saw Queenie."

"How does she fare?"

Phillip nodded toward the house. "You may ask her when you see her."

"She is here?" Billy's green eyes widened with surprise.

"She would not miss this event and will stay until Emma is back on her feet."

"Bold."

"Indeed. I don't know who I fear more—her or Roseline. It may be that I will find myself at the cabin in the swamp."

Billy chuckled. "Come now. With the name you've made for yourself? They miss you and your boats in Kingston."

Phillip snorted. "They miss my money since I took everything and moved it back here. I have just acquired another fishing boat with Hidalgo investing in a third of it."

Billy gave a low whistle. "Another trusted and influential Spanish contact. You're a calculating one to be sure."

"One can't be too careful with war on the horizon."

"What have you heard?" Billy leaned forward with concern.

"Oh, no, nothing as of yet. Queenie says it will be a few years, a dozen or so. Pensacola is too tempting to the rest of the world to be left alone forever."

"Who does she think it will be?"

"The Americans." Phillip shrugged. "It makes no difference to me." He looked around. "I have made sure to secure connections with all of the flags sailing these waters. Emma and I will never leave these shores."

"I don't blame you," said Billy with an air of wistfulness. "What a home you have."

A sudden wail echoed from the window, and Phillip came to his feet. He stared, willing Roseline to come to the sill and motion him inside. After a few long seconds, he bent his knees to sit again, but before he could do so, Betsy came sailing out of the courtyard door. She hurried over as both men met her in the middle of the yard.

"The swamp witch says to come in," she whispered in a loud, clandestine tone. Billy laughed and thumped him on the back. Phillip lifted his gaze to the heavens, threw his friend an amused glance, and said, "Wait here."

He hurried inside, jumped every other stair, and rushed to the chambers he shared with his wife. Before he could knock, Queenie Oba flung open the door. A bright white apron was tied under her generous bosom. Her round eyes looked as wide as a fish's. "Why do you have to make so much noise, Phillip-boy? You sounded like a bear clomping up those stairs."

Phillip winced and made a show of putting a finger to his lips. His heart thumped in his ears in the quiet. Queenie pursed her mouth, widened the door, and allowed him to enter. Roseline swept by with a pitcher and stopped to kiss him on the cheek. He gave her a hurried smile and brushed past the bedpost to see Emma. She was lying on her back in her silk dressing gown with heaps of linens stacked over her. He realized one was a bundle in her arms.

"Emma," he mumbled with a catch in his throat. Her hair was down and shining like mahogany. She looked exhausted and pale, but there was a light in her eyes he'd never seen before. A grin tugged at his lips. "I don't know whether to kiss you or peek under the blanket."

"Do both," she suggested in a whisper.

The door clicked shut behind them. When Phillip looked, he saw that Roseline and Queenie had disappeared. He bit back a satisfied smile and turned to his wife. Tears of happiness glimmered in her eyes. He leaned down and kissed her lips, clinging to the familiar taste and smell of her. She let out a quiet sigh. "You still love me then, after all that noise?"

"As much and more for forever. You are well then? That was so much faster than I expected."

"Yes, I was lucky," Emma admitted. She chuckled. "I didn't feel lucky at the time, of course, but at least it didn't go on for days."

"Yes, boys are like that," Phillip guessed. "As you say, always in a hurry."

"I don't think I would have managed without Queenie." Emma pressed her lips together then shyly raised the bundle in her arms. "We did quite well, Phillip."

"We have done quite well, you and I." He kissed her again on the forehead with a heart thumping in anticipation then glanced down. "For two chipped seashells that washed up on the shore with nowhere else to go."

Emma shifted the blanket off the head of a beautiful round face with dark eyes. "Well, this little shell is perfect and not going anywhere."

Phillip couldn't help himself even though Queenie had told him he was not to touch. He cupped his hand over the soft down feathering the newborn's crown. It was as bright as oranges. "My," he said in a strangled voice, "it looks like Master Oakley has his father's hair."

Emma giggled softly. "Queenie says it will fall out and come back darker like yours. And her blue eyes will turn, too, and become brown like mine."

"Her?" Phillip looked up in surprise.

"Oh, yes," Emma grinned. "Didn't anyone tell you? Chekilli's prediction was wrong, and Queenie Oba wins again. I'm sorry you won't have another sailor to add to your crew."

"No cabin boy, huh?" He shrugged and reached out his hands. "Can I hold the little thing then? My little Emma?"

"Of course." Emma passed him the tiny life that felt as light as a cloud in his arms. "But you must not call her 'Little Emma' as you've threatened to do."

"Why, what shall I call her then?"

Phillip's wife—woman, mother of his child and most trusted confidant—leaned closer and with a sly grin, announced, "Since we made a deal that I will name the girls, then she will be our little Mary Alice, but of course, this one stays in Pensacola."

The End

More Books
by Danielle Thorne

Historical
The Privateer of San Madrid
A Pirate at Pembroke
Proper Attire
Josette
Gentlemen of the Coast Book 1: A Smuggler's Heart
Gentlemen of the Coast Book 2: A Captain's Bride

Holiday
Brushstrokes and Blessings
Henry's Holiday Charade
Garland's Christmas Romance
Valentine Gold

Contemporary
His Daughter's Prayer (Love Inspired®)
Turtle Soup
By Heart and Compass
Death Cheater
Cheated

About the Author

DANIELLE THORNE WRITES historical and contemporary romance from south of Atlanta, Georgia. Married for thirty years to the same fellow, she's the mother of four boys, two daughters-in-law, and she has two grandbabies. There are also cats involved.

Danielle is a graduate of Ricks College and BYU-Idaho. Besides writing pursuits, she's active in her church and community. Free time is filled with books, movies, too much yardwork, and not enough wandering the country or cruising the beautiful, blue seas. She's worked as an editor for Solstice and Desert Breeze Publishing and is the author of non-fiction for young adults.

Her first book with Harlequin's Love Inspired line will be out July 2020.

KEEP IN TOUCH!
Visit www.daniellethorne.com to sign up for Danielle's newsletter,
and click the *About Me* page for social media links to connect.

---

[1] ARNADE CHARLES W. *The Florida Historical Quarterly. Volume Xxxvii January-April¹, 1959 Numbers 3 And 4*. Web. 4 August 2020

Made in the USA
Las Vegas, NV
04 May 2024